My Sweet Vermont

Sara J. Kuhrman

SOVEREIGN PUBLISHERS

Erie, Pennsylvania

DEDICATION

This book is dedicated to my wonderful mother, Rhonda Kuhrman. You have made everything possible for me.

ALSO BY SARA J. KUHRMAN:

Lost & Found

The Hallowed Halls

Gaze the Night*

Amethyst Highlands*

Tempest's Bachelor*

*publication still pending

Chapter One

    It was a rainy, dull Thursday afternoon, nearing 4:35 PM, and Araminta Cullen was hard at work behind her desk, doing calculations for the real estate closing that was coming up in a few days. After punching in a particularly long sequence of numbers into her adding machine, Mindy took a pause and lifted her head, brushing a wisp of her light-brown hair behind her ear and leaned back in her chair, stretching her sore back muscles. Looking out the window, Mindy's contemplative expression deepened into a frown. The view from her office window was quite unspectacular, even unsightly. The bank in which she worked was situated on the third floor of an office complex, looking out over a moderately busy hill street, and neighbored by identical gray office buildings and rundown tenements in the near distance. The scenery was unattractive as it was, but it was much worse when it was raining. *It's always damned raining,* Mindy thought to herself with frustration. Though it was the middle of August in a crowded New Jersey city, no one would ever guess. The hill street was slicked with rain, cars moving slowly up and down the incline like tepid molasses. The trees in the distance bowed under the weight of the strong wind, which flattened the leaves to look like large clumps of broccoli. Tired of what she was seeing, Mindy turned away from the window and re-focused on her work with a tired sigh. She made adequate money as a banker, but sometimes her work could get so boring. She worked hard for another fifteen or twenty minutes, looking over the frames of her cat's-eye glasses at the documents, red pen in hand, until she heard a voice from the doorway of her office.

"Hey, workaholic, boss says you can be done for the day, everybody's going home."

Mindy looked up with irritation to see Sam Mylan, her neighboring banker, smirking cockily at her, leaning casually against the doorframe. He was the epitome of the smug, polished banker, looking too sharp in his pinstripe suit, all the way down to his shined shoes. He had buzzed black hair and a square face, his hazel eyes always full of smug satisfaction. He seemed to have a thing for Mindy, and she never gave him the time of day.

"Okay," Mindy responded tiredly. "I suppose I could cut out, I've got laundry to do at home."

Ignoring Sam, who was still standing in the doorway, Mindy stood up and slipped on her gray windbreaker jacket and began packing folders into her simple brown briefcase. Laying the case on her desk, she fastened the buckles with a crisp *snap.* "Wanna join me for a drink tonight?" Sam persisted. "I'm heading over to Junior's Pub with the guys, but if you want, it can be just you and me." He shot her a wink. "Whaddaya say, Mindy?"

Mindy hoisted the case up into carrying position and strode for the door of her office, flicking out the lights with her free hand. "No thanks," she said coolly, firmly. "Like I said, it's laundry day."

Mindy locked up her office and strode across the foyer toward the elevator, briefcase under her arm. She simply tolerated Sam, who trailed behind her like an annoying insect, still talking.

"I bet the laundry can't do you like I could," Sam joked, laughing at his own lascivious comment as they stepped into the elevator. "Or are you just frightened by my manliness?"

Mindy glared at him, her pale blue-gray eyes flashing sharply. "Cut it out, Sam," she warned. "It's been a long day and I don't need shit from you."

Even though Sam towered over Mindy, the menacing look in her eyes seemed to shut him up. Moodily, he closed his mouth and turned to the side, flicking an invisible piece of lint from his suit coat.

"Sorry, that was out of line," he apologized grudgingly, giving her an almost disgusted look as the elevator reached the ground floor and the doors opened with a cheerful *ding*.

Mindy lifted her attaché case and regarded him coolly. "I've already forgotten about it," she answered tiredly, refusing to let him get under her skin. "See you tomorrow."

With that, Mindy continued at her brisk pace across the main lobby, her high heels rapping on the tile floor. Looking out the glass-front doors of the building, she was relieved to see that the rain had let up, leaving only residual drops dripping from the wet branches of the trees. Pulling up her hood, Mindy pushed the door open and headed across the wet parking lot to her beat-up silver sedan, which was parked in the corner space. Sighing, Mindy opened her car and tossed her briefcase into the passenger seat, sliding into her own seat and closing the door. Once she was in her car, away from the stressful day of work, Mindy took a calming breath and fastened her seatbelt and started the ignition. She peeled out of the parking lot and cranked up the radio, bobbing her head as her favorite alternative-rock band roared their way through the first track on their new album.

Slightly aggravated by the rush-hour traffic, Mindy sat at a particularly long stop light, drumming her pale, slim fingers on the steering wheel and bobbing her head to the thumping bass that was shaking her car. Every heavy guitar riff and screaming verse helped to diffuse the tension that had been building up all day long. As the light changed to green, Mindy tromped down on the accelerator and shot through the intersection. It wasn't very far from the bank to the dingy flat where Mindy lived, but the traffic slowed the drive to twenty minutes.

Finally, Mindy turned down a narrow side street and approached the weathered cinderblock duplex that she called her home. With a weary sigh, she parked across the street and hoisted up her briefcase, looking both ways before crossing the road in her usual brisk, efficient manner. Reaching her door, Mindy fished through her pocket and pulled out an archaic brass key, twisting it in the lock and pushing the door open.

When Mindy stepped inside her apartment, it appeared as it always did, dark and silent, with the slight smell of dusty carpet. Mindy set down her briefcase with a *thump* and shed her coat, crossing the room with a pensive expression to open the windows. Once the windows were opened, she headed to her bedroom to change her clothes. As she passed by the full-length mirror on her wall, she paused to take a look at herself.

As she gazed at her reflection, she saw a slim, pale young woman, only twenty-seven but aged by work and her monotonous, single life. *What a waste, to become old before my time,* she thought, looking at herself sorrowfully. Though her brow was wrinkled with pensive discontent, she was actually quite beautiful in a plain way. Her skin was pale and flawless, with only a distinct mole next to her wry pink lips. Her hair was light brown and wavy, held back by a hairclip, with dangling tendrils framing her face. Her eyes, pale bluish-gray, were long-lashed and full of quiet, dry wit behind her cat's eye glasses. Softly, she placed her hands on her hips and ran them over her figure, turning sideways to examine her form. Her build was slim but hard, compact. Her chest was pretty flat but her hips had the tiniest bit of flair that added intrigue to her brisk gait. Dressed in a white, form-fitting V-neck shirt, sleek black slacks and moderate heels, she looked the part of the quiet, conservative banker, no frills and no nonsense.

Done with her self-evaluation, Mindy stripped off her work clothes and matching beige lingerie; tossed them into the laundry hamper. After freshening up, Mindy changed into a comfortable navy-blue cotton T-shirt, running shorts and sneakers. Releasing her hair from the clip, she tossed it back in a ponytail, and headed off to collect the laundry to take to the laundromat down the street, deciding to hit the gym while she was waiting, pass some time and blow off some steam before returning home to her frozen dinner accompanied by the evening news.

Chapter Two

As the watery light of dawn began to spread across the night sky, Mindy was still asleep, with her arms flung out to the side and her hair messy, undone from the bun she had tied it back in. Her alarm clock began to beep noisily and Mindy stirred, letting out a soft murmur of discontent as she was wrenched from her ambiguous dreams.

Blinking groggily, Mindy sat up in bed and frowned at the little black clock, which was still beeping and displaying a flashing screen of 5:56 AM. Annoyed, she took a swipe at the snooze button and it fell silent. Unfortunately, though, Mindy knew that she couldn't afford to snooze. The bank opened at 7:30 and she often got to work early to keep up with the multitude of papers that flooded her desk every day.

With her bare feet landing softly on the hardwood floor in her bedroom, Mindy padded over to the window and parted the plain white curtains to let in the murky, dishwater-colored morning light. Sighing heavily, Mindy stretched deeply and yawned, committing to a few minutes of aerobic exercises to wake up and prevent stiffness later in the day. To accompany her brief exercises, she turned up her bedside radio for some beat-heavy dance music to get herself in the mood.

After a ten minute intense aerobic workout, Mindy turned off the music and headed to the shower, fragments of the songs she played still looping through her head. As she brushed her teeth and stood under the lukewarm water, she realized that dance music at 6AM was the only way she could possibly wrench herself out of bed. She wasn't a morning person by nature but her job forced her to be. It was only weekends that she was allowed the luxury of spending half the day sprawled out on her old, creaky double bed, which was nothing more than a glorified cot. Though Mindy had worked her way up to a position with a good salary, she saved most of her money, not knowing why she did. It was almost as if something was mounting in her future, and she was saving it for a special occasion.

Getting dressed for work took maybe ten minutes, as Mindy was very efficient. Today she chose a short-sleeved blue blouse and another pair of form-fitting black slacks, nylon knee-highs and her well-worn black pumps. Running a comb through her hair, she pinned it up in a clip again, the dangling strands framing her face and giving it a sharper, more angular look that she liked. Then, she placed her glasses on the bridge of her nose, grabbed her briefcase, and of course, umbrella, and headed out the door, checking her watch as she left her apartment.

On the way to work, Mindy swung through the drive-thru of the closest cheap fast-food restaurant and ordered a triple-shot macchiato and a milkshake, which would be her breakfast. Mindy's favorite foods were milkshakes, soup, and PBJ sandwiches, anything canned, packaged, or instant. As busy as she was, these were all fast options. She hadn't eaten a real fresh meal in years.

With her briefcase in one hand and a drink carrier in the other, Mindy stepped out of her car in the parking lot of the bank building, doing a balancing act as she locked her car and walked briskly toward the door. Luckily, a man held it open for her and she thanked him, though his eyes were clearly on the curve of her hips.

Mindy hurried to the elevator, giving a hurried greeting to some of the tellers who were already setting up. She could feel them watching her with admiration, in awe of her quiet, curt demeanor. With a mirthless laugh, she pondered on why they would envy her, finding it rather dryly amusing. Was it because she was so thin? That was because she had suffered with anorexia and bulimia all throughout her teenage years, still being a painfully picky eater. Was it her crazy work ethic? That was because she was a full-on workaholic. Was it her beat-up brown briefcase? That thought made her smile. The old veteran briefcase really was a worthy source of envy.

The ride to the third floor was short, and soon the elevator doors opened with a crisp *ding.* Always pressed for time, Mindy made her way just as briskly toward her office. As she unlocked her door, still in thought, she heard a voice behind her.

"Morning, Miss Precision, got a lot of work today?"

Mindy didn't have to turn around to identify the voice's obnoxious owner. "Actually I do," she responded curtly, making her way into her office and flicking on the lights, taking a seat behind her computer desk. "Why don't you go start yours?"

Sam grinned, standing in the doorway. "Oh, Miss Cullen, you do amuse me," he said with a yawn. "Well, maybe I should go start my work. But want to go out for lunch?"

Mindy shook her head. "Nah, I'm just gonna stay here," she replied evenly, tonelessly turning him down again. Unable to help herself, she frowned at him over the frames of her glasses as he walked into her office uninvited. "When will you figure out that I'm a busy woman, and that no means no?"

Sam shrugged. "Maybe never," he replied with a lovelorn Fred Astaire-like wink. "See you later," he sang, walking out of her office once again.

Shaking her head, Mindy logged into her computer and checked her email. *Obnoxious prick,* she mumbled to herself as Sam left. She had no time for frivolity, and didn't appreciate his smug advances. Still, though, she refused to let it bother her, able to easily brush him off and get lost in her work. She knew that she was the best banker in the place, her numbers were spectacular. But when she checked her e-mail, there was a note from the vice president of the department to come see him at lunchtime. Mindy was confused, wondering what that could mean. She emailed back that she would, and was rather distracted for the rest of the day.

At lunchtime, Mindy waited apprehensively outside the vice president's office, nervously twisting her hands. Taking a shaky breath, she lifted her hand and knocked on the wooden door marked: <u>J. Carson Dean</u>, Vice President.

"Come in," came the muffled voice from within, and Mindy pushed the door open.

The vice president, a serious but kindly bespectacled gentleman, sat in his leather swivel chair with his hands clasped in front of him. He smiled when Mindy stepped in. "Ah, Araminta, take a seat," he gestured to the chair opposite his desk.

Mindy sat down and crossed her legs. "So, you wanted to see me, Mr. Dean?" she inquired, trying to sound professional and keep the nervousness out of her voice.

Mr. Dean nodded seriously. "I just wanted to have a talk with you and let you know that I found a big mistake in the loan papers you filled out for Collin Industries. This isn't how you usually work, Mindy. Is something wrong?"

Mindy shook her head. "Not that I know of," she responded, unable to keep her voice from cracking. "I've been trying so hard… in here at seven every day…" she broke off and a tear slipped down her cheek.

Mr. Dean handed her a tissue. "Stay calm," he told her. "We will get this fixed, but it can't happen again." He gave her a long, pensive look. "Perhaps you've been working too hard," he said finally, clasping his hands together in front of him. "Hard work is admirable, but unproductive if you make mistakes like this. Just a consideration."

Mindy was silent for a long moment before she nodded gravely. "Thanks for seeing me," she told him. "I'll go eat my lunch now."

Mr. Dean gave her a kindly but grave smile. "You're one of our best bankers, Mindy," he told her. "I'd like to see you get back in the game."

She bade him goodbye and left the office, but his words rang in her mind all day. *Big mistake. Working too hard. Unproductive.* Mindy was in panic mode, knowing that if she lost her high work ethic she would lose everything, because work was everything to her. At lunch hour she closed her door and put on some music to clear her mind while she ate her PBJ.

***

Later in the evening, Mindy had finished her errands and was back at home, reading a novel. With a sidelong glance in the direction of the telephone handset, she saw that it was 7PM already. Adjusting her glasses on the slender bridge of her nose, Mindy decided that it was time for dinner. It had certainly been a hell of a day, she thought. Being up from 5:56AM and going straight didn't leave one with much at the end of the day. Mindy didn't really want to give up her spot on the couch, but she knew that it would only get later and later if she didn't make her dinner soon.

With a weary sigh, Mindy pushed herself off of the couch and made her way across the faded beige carpet that blanketed her living room floor, the only sounds being the dull hum of traffic outside, the sound of her soft, shuffling footsteps, and the ticking of her mantel clock. As she took this in, Mindy realized just how lonely living alone could be. Most of the time she liked the peace and quiet, but sometimes her apartment could be too silent and sterile.

Cranking up her radio to diffuse the quiet, Mindy padded across the room and rounded the corner, stepping into her simple kitchenette. Her semblance of a kitchen was no fancier than the rest of her dwelling, with a worn tile floor, white walls, and all the essentials: stovetop countertop, microwave, coffee maker, refrigerator and freezer. Other than that, there wasn't much else; except for a couple of cheap prints she'd hung on the wall. As Mindy got out a pan and a can of soup, she saw her dish towel hanging up, a red and white checkered cloth with the words "Home Sweet Home" spelled out in embroidery. The piece of cheesy kitchenware had been a gift from her mother when she'd gotten her own place. Turning the towel over in her hands, Mindy mused that although she had lived in New Jersey for most of her life, it had never felt like a home. In fact, she had never felt anything for her town except resigned indifference and covert discontent.

Bobbing her head softly to the music emanating from the radio, Mindy set the towel down and opened a can of soup, pouring it into the pan and turning on the burner. While she waited for the soup to cook, Mindy made herself busy by emptying the dishwasher and loading the clean dishes into the cabinet.

Mindy's soup was done in a few minutes. This was exactly why she loved canned food. No prep, no mess, perfect for a jaded workaholic banker such as herself. Shutting off the burner, Mindy carried her soup bowl back into the living room, blowing on it slowly to cool it. As per nightly tradition, Mindy set her soup down, picked up the remote, and switched on the TV to the news channel.

Even as the news anchors blathered on, Mindy found herself unable to pay attention. She was still anxious and preoccupied with how things had gone down at work. As she took a sip of her water, Mindy frowned, trying to think about how she could get her work life back on track. Mr. Dean had told her that she might be working too hard, and that really bothered her. *What will I do now?* She thought to herself. She really didn't want to cut down her hours and didn't know how she might give herself a rest. Idly, her eyes flicked to the TV screen, where an ad for a luxurious Florida resort was playing. She considered a vacation, but seeing the fake sand and cheesy palm-tree theme, she knew she'd rather skip it and stay home. Hot weather made her irritable, so Mindy knew that she was definitely not going south, especially in the heat of the summer. With a frown, Mindy considered vacation destinations but nothing really stood out to her or seemed any better than where she was. With a frustrated sigh, Mindy decided that she would have to abandon the vacation idea and try to find another way to improve at work.

Abruptly, Mindy rose from the couch with a grim set to her mouth and made her way to the kitchen, where she deposited her dirty dishes in the sink, suddenly not hungry anymore. This thing with work was going to drive her crazy, she thought, trying for once just to push it out of her mind for the rest of the night.

Sighing again, Mindy tried to stop the tears from clouding her eyes, shaking her head in desperation. *Hot chocolate,* she thought, spying a long-forgotten carton of hot-chocolate mix shoved in the corner of the cabinet, next to the cookbook. *That's what I need. Hot chocolate with marshmallows and a good old movie.*

Feeling slightly better, Mindy reached for the hot chocolate, but it was just at the limit of her reach. She stood on her tiptoes and tried to grab it, but somehow ended up toppling the cookbook. "Damn it," she muttered, crouching down to pick up all of the flyaway papers that had gone airborne and were now scattered across the floor.

As she picked up all of the papers, she gave them a disinterested glance, stacking them back up. Just as she was about to return the sheaf of paper to the book, a stout, stiff paper caught her attention. Separating it from the pile, Mindy saw that it was a beautiful postcard with a picture of a lakeside city at sunset. Inscribed on the bottom in white letters, it read: *Burlington, Vermont.* Smiling, she gazed at the picture, almost hypnotized by how beautiful it looked. In her landlocked New Jersey town, she had never seen a lakeside sunset, except maybe in the movies. With a puzzled, wondering expression, she turned it over, trying to remember who she had gotten this from, but to her surprise it was only bore her address in slanted, scrawled penmanship, no name or message. "Hmm," she mused, figuring it was probably from one of her relatives during the postcard fad ten years ago. Shrugging, Mindy turned it back over and studied the glossy print. It was almost as if there were something magical about the picture, and the city where it was taken.

In a moment of clarity, the answer dawned on her. "Burlington," she breathed softly, a teary smile spreading across her pale, drawn face. "I'm going to Burlington!"

Now smiling radiantly, Mindy put the cookbook back and made herself a cup of hot chocolate, heading back to the living room with a new resolve: planning her trip. She knew that it might not be easy to get hotel reservations at such a short notice, but she was determined to try, because she'd never in her life felt anything like she had when she picked up the mysterious picture.

Chapter Three

The subsequent days before Mindy's trip were part of a colorful rush of madness: plane tickets, hotel reservations, suitcase packing, time-out slips at work, etc. First stop on Monday was Mr. Dean's office to fill out her vacation slip. Lunchtime had just barely started, and Mindy had a pause in her work, so she rose from her swivel chair, set her pen down, and exited her office, vacation request slip in her hand. With only the slightest twinge of apprehension, Mindy knocked on the vice president's door. Though she appeared calm, this meeting was a matter of life and death to her. She *had* to go on this trip; it was a beacon of irresistible hope in her otherwise dim future. As soon as she had been offered a window into Burlington, Vermont, she wanted nothing more than to surrender to her craving to walk through the door.

Deep in thought, Mindy was startled out of her reverie by the sound of Mr. Dean calling for her to come in. Taking a deep breath, Mindy pushed the door open and greeted the kindly vice president, who was sitting thoughtfully behind his desk. When he saw Mindy, he clasped his hands in front of him on his desk. "Ah, Mindy," he said pleasantly, inviting her to sit down. "What can I do for you today?"

Mindy smiled back at him and slid her vacation slip across his desk. "Well, I listened to what you said yesterday, about working too hard, and I decided I'd like to take a vacation," she told him.

Mr. Dean pondered her words, and drew his hand to his chin, thinking. "Well, I suppose," he answered finally. "How long would you propose to be gone?"

Mindy tried to appear confident. "I'd like to go for a month," she said, trying to keep the anxiousness from her voice. "I hope that's okay with you, this trip is very important to me."

Mr. Dean frowned. "I don't know, Araminta. There will be a lot of work over a month. I don't want you to fall behind again."

Mindy bit her lip. "I know," she replied shakily. She looked at him pleadingly. "But I haven't had a vacation in years, Mr. Dean. This is the opportunity for me to rejuvenate myself."

Mr. Dean thought for a long moment. Finally, he spoke. "Okay," he replied, his tone still reserved. "When would you like to go?"

"Monday, if possible," Mindy told him. "I promise I'll get caught up before I go."

He nodded. "Yes, make sure you stay caught up. I'll enter the time in now."

Mindy's nervous expression relaxed into a beaming smile. "Thank you so much, Mr. Dean," she exclaimed. "Thanks for everything."

Mr. Dean smiled at her exuberance. "You're welcome," he answered. "Take care of yourself now."

"You too, thanks," Mindy practically sang as she sailed out of his office.

Feeling as light as air, Mindy strutted back to her office, beginning to see her life in a new light. Even from a postcard picture, Mindy felt the vibrant aura of the city, just the faintest trace of it, emanating from the very concept of the city itself. It was so different than anything Mindy had ever experienced before, and she was further intrigued when she looked up additional pictures of Burlington, each one proving to be beautiful.

As Mindy was caught up in further thoughts of her vacation, she failed to notice that Sam had sidled up to her office doorway, his usual smirk adorning his face.

"So, did ya finally get some action last night or what?" his voice broke Mindy's concentration and she whipped around, giving him a quizzical stare.

"What?" Mindy wondered, crinkling her nose. "What are you talking about?"

"You know," Sam gave her a conspiratorial wink. "You're glowing, and you haven't even yelled at me yet today. He must have been good, huh?"

Mindy shook her head. "I haven't yelled at you yet because I've lacked an opportunity," she replied wryly. "And I'm just looking forward to my vacation."

"Your *what*?" Sam gasped, nearly dropping the stack of folders he was carrying. "You? On vacation? Since when?"

"I put in my time today," Mindy answered calmly.

"And how…" Sam was still stammering. "How long will you be gone?"

"A month," Mindy replied, with her back to him. "I leave on Sunday."

Sam's only response was a muffled comment about her having gone bonkers. Still shaking his head, he managed a shaky, "I'm going to lunch," and walked out of her office, looking like he was on the verge of losing his sanity.

After he left, Mindy chuckled to herself. *Dang,* she thought. *I would have gone on vacation earlier if I knew it would freak him out so much. Maybe he'd leave me alone.* Taking a forkful of her PBJ sandwich that she had cut into pieces, Mindy chewed thoughtfully as she reviewed the spreadsheet on the computer in front of her. So far it had been quite successful. She only hoped the rest of the trip would be that easy.

Chapter Four

The week went by so quickly that Mindy could barely remember experiencing it, such a rush of planning for her trip that she barely had time to breathe. But, finally, it was Sunday morning of her big trip.

Mindy was lying in her bed, still fast asleep, with her arms flung out to the side and her wayward, wavy brown hair fanned out all across her pillow. Through the crack in the curtains, the dishwater-gray light of another overcast New Jersey morning filtered into her darkened room. As a stray ray of light shone across Mindy's pale, closed eyes, she stirred in her sleep and began to wake up.

Blinking groggily, Mindy glanced at the alarm clock beside her bed and saw that it was only a few minutes after seven. Rubbing the sleep out of her eyes, Mindy tossed back the covers and rose, wanting to be ready in time for her 1:00 PM flight from Newark to Burlington. Looking forward to her trip, Mindy efficiently made her way into the bathroom to clean up. She showered and brushed her teeth, and when she came back into her bedroom she nearly put on her work clothes by rote habit. *I won't need these today,* Mindy thought to herself with a smile as she picked up her worn black pumps and put them back in the closet. Instead, she chose to dress in a soft, form-fitting periwinkle V-neck t-shirt, khaki shorts, gray bobby socks and her favorite pair of running sneakers. Also, she put on her sterling-silver cross necklace and tossed her unruly brown hair back in a ponytail. Looking at her reflection in the mirror, Mindy thought that she looked pretty good. The clothes she picked clung to her slim, flat form in all the right places and showed off her strong legs. The periwinkle color accented her pale eyes and her glasses added an intriguing curve to her sharp-angled face. Satisfied with how she looked, Mindy stooped down to check her suitcase and make sure everything was in place. She was an efficient traveler, packed light for heavy impact. In her maroon duffel bag she had brought maybe seven outfits, underwear, socks, shoes, and an economy-size bag of travel toiletries. The only other thing she brought was her purse, which she stuffed the rest of her things in.

Satisfied again with her packing, Mindy made her bed and went about shutting things down in her apartment, making the already sterile space seem as austere as a doctor's office. Everything was packed up and turned off, retired, but Mindy liked it that way.

Feeling energized, Mindy slipped her purse over her shoulder and lifted her duffel bag, heading out the door of her apartment and locking it behind her. Then, she packed her duffel bag into the backseat of her car and hopped into the driver's seat. Cranking up her radio, she closed the door and backed out of her driveway, knowing that was the last time she would see her beat-up duplex in a month. Liberated, Mindy sang along with her music as she pulled into the drive-thru restaurant-bakery place on the corner of the street.

When she arrived at the window, Mindy ordered a large black coffee and a cinnamon twist, handing a ten-dollar bill in through the window. Thanking the boy for the change, Mindy took the bag and the money and parked in the parking lot, deciding to stop and eat her breakfast before she tried the near-impossible feat of navigating downtown traffic to the airport. When she was finished, Mindy wiped her face and pulled out of the lot, deciding to brave the daunting ride to the airport.

The traffic was nearly bumper-to-bumper all the way into the city, and Mindy found herself growing tired. But finally, after what seemed like ages of sitting in parked traffic with her turn signal on, Mindy was able to get a ticket and make it into the parking lot of the airport. Cutting her motor, Mindy stepped out and hefted her duffel bag onto her shoulder, making her way towards the massive terminal.

As she stared down the giant building, Mindy couldn't help but to feel a twinge of apprehension tingle along her nerves. This was the first time she had ever been out of the state, or the city, except for when she was a baby, which she didn't remember. Shaking her head to disperse the anxiety, Mindy squared her shoulders and continued on towards the great revolving doors. *I can do this,* Mindy told herself. *I'm going to Burlington.* Reaching into her purse, Mindy extracted the folded postcard and studied it, her face lighting up as she remembered why she wanted to go. Smiling again, she tucked the majestic scene back into her purse and continued on, feeling less nervous.

When she reached the massive revolving door, she shifted her bag in her hands and proceeded through, being spit out into the vast, teeming terminal. Inside, people milled about right and left, shouting greetings to each other, purchasing tickets, and being scanned through security. Willing herself not to be freaked out by the great amount of people, Mindy did what she needed to do and went to the counter to get a baggage ticket. Once the paper was secure in her hands, she returned to the lobby to take a seat until it was time to go through security.

As Mindy waited in the airport, she pulled out a book and tried to tune out the surrounding chaos. She was halfway into a chapter when a deep male voice above her broke into her reverie. "Excuse me," a man boomed, and Mindy jumped, clumsily slamming her book shut. Annoyed at having been disturbed, she squinted up at the hulking figure above her, able to make out a tall, broad-shouldered man in a black pin-striped suit. He had long hair pulled back into a low ponytail, ugly brown eyes, and an unsightly smattering of stubble on his chin.

"May I help you?" Mindy asked him quizzically, wondering if he just needed directions to the restroom or something.

"Are you Araminta Cullen?" the man enquired.

Mindy frowned and drew back a little bit, reaching protectively for her purse. "I am," she replied warily. "Who are you?"

The man smiled, but to Mindy it looked more like a leer. "Perfect," he answered congenially, sinking down into the chair beside her. "My name is Troy Haverman. I will be heading up your department at the bank while you're on vacation," he explained. "You know, we can't have headless departments running around."

Mindy stared at the large, smirking man, wondering if he was for real. He didn't look like a banker, except maybe for his pin-striped suit. "Is this some kind of joke?" she demanded, her eyes flashing with irritation.

But Troy Haverman reached into his pants pocket and withdrew his business card, indicating that he was the assistant head of the Commercial Finance department. "I'll be doubling my workload while you're gone," he explained.

"I see," she replied flatly. "I have left notes on how I want everything done. Mr. Dean should be able to answer any questions."

The man didn't seem to be fazed by her cold shoulder. Instead, he smiled again. "Very professional of you, Miss Cullen," he drawled sardonically. "I'm sure I will fit in just fine."

Assuming that the conversation was over, Mindy nodded and reopened her book to continue reading. But to her annoyance, the man didn't make any move to leave. "Where are you vacationing to?" he wondered in an overly genial tone.

Mindy didn't look up. "Essex," she lied briskly, not feeling the need to disclose her exact whereabouts to this bothersome stranger.

"I've never been there," her annoying seatmate continued, his gaze roaming lasciviously over her slim figure. "What's it like?"

"Great," Mindy said brusquely, getting thoroughly irritated by the man's intrusive comments. With her pale eyes flashing, she set her book down and scathed him with a direct glare. "Exactly what, Mr. Haverman, does my vacation destination have to do with your fill-in work?"

The man chuckled. "I was warned that you'd be cold," he commented, still seeming amused. "But you can call me Troy."

Looking at her watch, Mindy rose from her seat. She wanted to be away from him. "Excuse me, *Mr. Haverman.* My flight is waiting. Consult my notes if you have questions."

With that, Mindy strode off to go deposit her baggage and get scanned through security. Shaking her head, she bit off a mirthless laugh. *Stupid clod,* she thought to herself. Men could be so irritating sometimes, especially the ones she worked with. Just where did this dude get off following her to the airport to make small talk with her? Mindy found the encounter quite creepy and unprofessional. But if Dean had asked him to take over her position, he must not be too dimwitted. What Mindy didn't understand is why sleazy men felt that they had the license to hit on her. *What is it about me that says, "Single and ready?"* Mindy wondered. She had snuffed out that part of her like the cigarettes she had smoked when she was seventeen years old. Araminta Cullen didn't date. She worked.

Pushing these bothersome thoughts from her mind, Mindy focused on her vacation and got in line to go through security, trying to blank her mind as her baggage was scanned and she barely flinched as the TSA officer patted down her and her belongings.

Once that whole ordeal was over, it was finally time to board. A pleasant stewardess ushered the passengers onto the plane, and Mindy found her seat on the aisle. Mindy was worried about who her seatmate might be, but a businessman with a laptop and headphones came to sit next to her, only nodding a greeting.

Mindy blew out a sigh of relief. Her seatmate looked thoroughly preoccupied with his work, unlikely to make annoying small talk. Already this vacation was looking good.

Pulling out her phone, Mindy put her own headphones on and turned the volume up, blasting heavy rock music in her ears and bobbing her head to the screeching guitar riffs. Then, she took out her book and continued reading where she had left off.

The flight was about two hours, give or take, and was generally pretty smooth. Before Mindy knew it, the captain was announcing landing time. Mindy watched out the window as they swept over wide, blue Lake Champlain, drawing nearer to the glimmering city until they touched down at its core, the Burlington International Airport. It took Mindy some time to debark and collect her luggage, but she was glad to be there. Stopping at a kiosk, she studied a flyer that listed the hours for the ferry across the lake. Recalling the glimpse of beauty she'd seen above, she wanted to experience Burlington for the first time again, see it from the water.

Though Mindy still had her luggage, she hailed a taxi anyway, she couldn't wait. The driver, a kindly older man, smiled at her and asked her where she wanted to go.

Mindy smiled. "I know this sounds silly, but it's my first time here, and I want to take the ferry across the lake and back."

"Absolutely," the driver replied genially. "I'd do the same."

The ferry dock was only a short distance from the airport. As they drove down to the shore, Mindy was astounded by the beauty of the lake. At the booth, the attendant took their tickets when the ferry came and the taxi drove onto the ramp. As the ferry started pulling away from the dock, Mindy noticed other passengers getting out of their cars and told the taxi driver that she would like to step out as well. He nodded and rolled down his window, taking in the breeze.

Feeling liberated, Mindy grabbed her purse and ascended the stairs to the second tier of the boat, sighing with pleasure as she scanned her surroundings. The sun was shining brilliantly, unlike anything Mindy had ever seen in New Jersey. The air was clear and fresh and gulls swooped and dived overhead, looking for fish. Below, the waves slapped rhythmically against the sides of the boat as fish danced mysteriously beneath the surface. On the way up, Mindy studied the surrounding mountains on the other side of the lake, intrigued by the bucolic, serene wilderness. There were a few farmhouses nestled in the bluish-green hills, and Mindy imagined what it would be like to live up there.

After a half hour, the ferry docked at Essex and let off passengers. Then, when they were back underway, the ship turned around and headed back to Burlington. The view was even more breathtaking than Mindy expected. She gasped in awe as she noticed that the entire city was shimmering, glowing almost blindingly in the late-afternoon sun. It seemed to be beckoning to her, radiating powerful waves of magic from its center. She felt like she was seeing it for the first time, completely entranced by the mystical city ahead of her.

Up on the deck of the ferry, with the wind streaming freely through her wavy brown hair as the ship rapidly approached paradise, Mindy realized that she had never been truly happy until that day.

Chapter Five

Mindy was so caught up in the hypnotizing bliss of the ferry ride that she barely noticed how close they were to the dock. As her golden city loomed before her, she took one more look and scurried below to get back into her cab. The cabdriver, who was also enjoying the scenery, nodded to her and they got back into the vehicle.

With a slow grinding sound of the motors, the massive boat pulled up to the dock and two blond, strong crewmen reached out to moor it to the posts along the dock. Once the ship was settled, the gates were open and they began directing traffic off onto the ramp. As the driver pressed down the gas pedal and they touched down on dry land, the driver turned to Mindy. "Welcome to Burlington, once again," he told her with a cheerful smile.

Mindy smiled back at the kindly older driver and thanked him, feeling a rush of tingling interest course through her as the reality hit home: she was in Burlington! Other than her brief landing at the airport, this was her first time seeing the city up close. Running a hand through her messy, wavy, light brown hair, Mindy sighed with pleasure and rolled down her window, letting a gust of the fresh lake breeze wash over her. *This is it,* she thought to herself; the satisfaction she had never felt and always longed for.

"Wow, it's magnificent," Mindy breathed, taking in the picturesque buildings and glittering waterfront. "So beautiful."

The driver nodded. "Indeed it is, Miss, it's captivating. Where should I take you now?"

Mindy smiled. "Back to the airport, please. I got so caught up in the ferry ride that I forgot about renting a car."

The driver nodded again. "Sure," he replied, and they drove along the main road to the airport. Next to the terminal was the car rental place. "Well, here we are," the driver announced, pulling up in front of the place. Mindy collected her bags from the backseat and paid the driver, thanking him for taking her on the ferry roundtrip. He smiled and said that he enjoyed the view, and also wished her good luck on her trip.

After Mindy had left the cab, she hoisted her duffel bag up and made her way through the automatic doors. She approached the desk and inquired about renting a car. The clerk wasn't personable but was very efficient, and she asked for Mindy's driver's license. Mindy showed it to her and the clerk slid a form across the desk. It didn't take too long to fill out, and when the transaction was complete, Mindy was handed a set of keys with a numbered tag attached. "Go out those doors; the lot is to your left. Look for the car with the matching number," the clerk directed her.

Mindy thanked the woman and followed the directions, heading out the doors and scanning the lot for car number 4309. Finally, she found it; a relatively new-looking compact dark-gray sedan. Nodding with approval, Mindy opened it up and found that though the car wasn't anything special, it was better than what she had at home. Tossing her bags in the backseat, Mindy climbed into the car and pulled out the crumpled sheet of paper that had the directions to her hotel. The place was called Rose Hill Inn and Suites, and they offered good deals for long-term guests. Fortunately, Mindy had called ahead and they were able to book her a room for the entire month.

Once she had a fair idea of where she should go Mindy thoughtfully put her car in reverse and backed slowly out of the parking lot, just thinking about how glad she was to be on vacation.

As she pulled out of the lot, she rolled down the windows to let in the fresh mountain air. *Ah,* she breathed. *Burlington is so beautiful.* The street was a little bit more crowded than she expected, but here in the city of paradise, Mindy didn't seem to mind. The hotel wasn't too far away, maybe a fifteen minute drive. Following the directions she had written down on the map, she flicked on her turn signal and turned off of the main road onto a side street. Up ahead on the left was her hotel, a four-story beige building with wide windows and an old creaky sign that proclaimed it the Rose Hill Inn. Perplexed by the vintage sign and clearly newer building, Mindy entered the driveway and parked in the parking lot.

With her single bag weighing down on her slim shoulders, Mindy strode purposefully to the doors of the hotel, though she paused slightly to look around at the hotel's plants and shrubbery. As she stepped through the sliding door, Mindy found herself in a pleasantly furnished lobby with a large dining room through glass doors ahead. Turning left, she approached the desk.

The desk clerk, a pleasant-faced college girl, looked up and smiled brightly at Mindy. "Hi, welcome to Rose Hill Inn! Are you here to check in?"

Mindy smiled back; pleased that everyone in town so far was so friendly. "Yes, I am," she responded. "My name is Araminta Cullen; I am reserving a suite for a month."

The girl looked something up on the computer before she smiled at Mindy again and handed her a room key. "Ah, yes, Ms. Cullen. You are in room 301. If you need anything at all, just dial zero."

"I will," Mindy replied. "Thank you."

"Hope you enjoy your stay," the girl told her. "It's such a lovely city. You'll be glad you're here."

"I am," Mindy responded. "I've never been anywhere like this before."

"There's no place like Burlington," the girl agreed. "There's so much to see." Just then, the phone rang. "Have a good evening, Ms. Cullen, I enjoyed talking to you," she called, waving as Mindy turned away.

Mindy smiled. "Thanks, you too."

After she finished talking with the desk clerk, Mindy picked up her bag and key and walked toward the elevator, stepping in and pressing the button for the third floor.

Mindy waited while the elevator glided smoothly up three floors and deposited her in a clean space with hardwood floors. Looking around, Mindy shifted her bag on her shoulder and turned left, following the sign that led to rooms 300-315. The hallway was dimly lit and done up in blue and brown carpet with picture windows on either end of the corridor. Mindy located her room at the end of the eastern wing, the dark brown door marked 301. Reaching into her pocket, Mindy drew out her key card and slid it in the slot. A moment later, the light flashed green, and with a heavy click, Mindy opened the door to her new home.

Mindy was impressed as she stepped into her room, taking it in slowly. The décor was plain but quaint. The walls were cream-colored and the rug was beige, with a painting of a beach on the wall. There was a pale blue couch by the window and a TV. Also in the sitting room was a sparse but sleek kitchenette, with cabinets and a refrigerator, dishwasher, sink, and stovetop. There was also a small table for meals.

Perfect, Mindy thought as she opened the double doors to the bedroom. Inside the bedroom, there were two pale blue double beds, the same beige carpeting, and white curtains. To the left was the door to the bathroom. At the window, the late-afternoon sun beamed in through the curtains, creating an orange glow. Mindy set her bag down between the beds, unsure of which one she wanted to sleep in. On one hand, if she had to go to the bathroom in the middle of the night, the one to the left would be closer. But on the other hand, the other was closer to the window and it had a pretty view of the terrace. After several moments of vacillation, Mindy decided on the bed closer to the window, but the side closer to the desk. Satisfied with her decision, Mindy set her bag down and checked the bedside clock, which proclaimed it to be 6:15 PM.

With a light sigh, Mindy sat down on her bed and opened her duffel bag, trying to decide what she should do next. At the bottom of the bag, she came across her ruffled black one-piece bathing suit. Mindy lifted it out and decided that she could use a relaxing swim after the day's long travel. Mindy shed her clothes and laid them on the bed, pulling on her black suit. Carefully, she removed her cat's-eye glasses and jewelry and set the items on her light stand. Then, she twisted her light brown hair up into a bun and put her clothes back on over her suit to go down to the pool. Taking her room key, Mindy left her room and made sure the door was locked firmly before she headed to the bank of elevators down the quiet hallway.

Once she had arrived at the first floor, Mindy followed the sign that led to the pool. The walkway was floor-to-ceiling glass, alongside the pretty outside terrace. Off to the side was a glass door with a key card scanner. Mindy turned left and opened the door with her key, stepping into the relaxing pool room. The pool itself was very clean, though rather unspectacular. But what made it beautiful was the same outside terrace view that lined the hallway. *What a pretty place,* Mindy thought to herself as the late-afternoon sun glowed orange through the glass windows, the rays dancing off the surface of the water. Setting her things down on the chair, Mindy was glad to see that the only other person in the pool was a quiet, older businessman who seemed to be doing some sort of meditation. Mindy stripped off her shirt and shorts, and was taken aback by her reflection in the mirror behind her, how good she looked. The black bathing suit skimmed over the curve of her hips and outlined her slim waist and long, strong legs. Her skin was pale and unblemished, and the top emphasized the very minimal cleavage that she possessed. This vision saddened Mindy slightly, that she had thrown away so many years of her life working herself nearly to death. She hadn't dated since she was seventeen, and it was doubtful as to whether she'd ever been in love, except a brief and painful yearning for a man who hadn't known or cared whether she existed.

Shaking her head to clear out these unpleasant thoughts, Mindy took off her shoes and dipped her toes into the pool, feeling the clean, warm water. A heated pool was exactly what Mindy needed after a stressful day of airplanes, airports, taxis, and traveling. With a hand delicately on the handrail, Mindy lowered herself into the water and sighed, stretching luxuriously as she swam out into the middle of the pool.

"Peaceful, isn't it?" the deep, quiet male voice interrupted Mindy's thoughts and she opened her eyes, still making lazy circles in the water with her arms. Looking over, she saw the meditating businessman smiling at her.

"Definitely," Mindy agreed, returning the man's kind smile. "The whole city is so lovely, and I've only been here a few hours."

The handsome gray-haired man raised his eyebrows. "Where're you from?" he wondered.

"That's a good question," Mindy replied quietly. "I was born in Montana, but never got to see it. I've lived mostly in New Jersey, but it isn't my home. The only place I've ever felt at home is here."

"I agree," the businessman answered. "I always stay here on my travel trips as long as possible. I'm scheduled for New Jersey next. How is it?"

"Well, my town is awful," Mindy said frankly. "I don't know about the rest of it, but don't bother with the Newark area."

To her surprise, the man laughed. "At least you're honest," he chuckled. "I'll consider myself well-warned."

After a few minutes of chatting with the man, Mindy found that he was quite pleasant, albeit a bit boring. When they finished their conversation, they lapsed into silence and the man climbed out of the pool.

"It was nice talking to you," he commented as he toweled off and packed up his things. "And if you hate your town that much, don't go back."

Mindy thanked him, and after he left, she pondered his words. *Don't go back.* The concept was thrilling to her, novel. His words echoed in her mind as she swam lazy laps and soaked her stress away, staying in the pool so long that she was startled when she noticed the sun going down.

With a furrowed brow, Mindy decided to get out, finding herself to be wet and shivering in the cool air. To fight the chill, Mindy toweled off and put her clothes back on over her bathing suit. Though she was quite wet and her shoes squeaked when she walked, she decided to head down the hallway and get something for dinner from the pantry at the front desk. She wrapped her hair in a towel turban and checked her watch, shocked that it was already quarter to nine. Suddenly ready to be out of the pool room, Mindy packed up quickly and departed for the lobby, her flip-flops making an obnoxious *squick-squick* noise on the tile floor.

Suppressing an immature laugh, Mindy approached the desk and ducked into the pantry on the side. Deciding to keep it simple, she picked out a can of easy mac-and-cheese, a sleeve of hot cocoa mix, and a banana, disappointed that they didn't have any soup to her liking. After she had picked out her meal, she went around to the desk and paid the clerk for the food before going back to her room.

By the time Mindy finished her shower, it was almost nine-thirty, and she was sitting on the couch with her meal of easy mac-and-cheese and black coffee courtesy of the coffeemaker in her room. To entertain herself while she ate, she turned on the news channel and kept it at a very low volume. Thinking about it, Mindy realized that this wasn't a whole lot different than her routine at home, except that she was much happier and more comfortable in Burlington. Setting down her dish when she had finished, Mindy lifted her mug of coffee and took a swig to wash it down. After she had cleaned up the dishes, Mindy changed into her PJ's, which consisted of a loose gray tank top and stretched-out athletic shorts. Before bed, she rose and looked out the window onto the darkened terrace, able to see the sparkling lights of the city not far from the hotel. Mindy was surprised by the intensity of the city's life force, humming through every particle in the air and wrapping her in a powerful field of warmth. The feeling stayed with Mindy as she made herself a cup of hot chocolate and got in bed to read, sliding her glasses up the bridge of her nose. It was unexplainable, like nothing she had ever felt before. It was almost like the essence of the city was seeping into her bones and cleansing all of her scars and disappointments away. As time went on, Mindy became tired and got up to use the bathroom and brush her teeth before taking her glasses off and sliding into bed. As soon as she turned the light off, Mindy sank into the soft mattress and fell deeply asleep.

Chapter Six

The next morning, Mindy was drifting in a state of semi-consciousness, eyes closed, her hair fanned out across her pillow. She lay perfectly still, aware of a blinding light above her, blinking rapidly to figure out where she was. As she slowly acclimated to her surroundings, Mindy realized that the blinding light was a crack of sunlight streaming in through the parted curtains. The sensation was so foreign to her that Mindy took a few moments to figure out what it was. Such a thing rarely ever happened in New Jersey, since it seemed to rain pretty much all the time. Feeling rested and completely content, Mindy stretched luxuriously, reveling in the softness of the mattress and the warmth of the sun on her face. Sitting up, she plowed a hand through her messy brown hair and checked the bedside clock, which indicated that it was 8:20 AM.

Thrilled that she could get up of her own accord and not by the persistent beeping of an alarm clock, Mindy rose and took her time as she opened the curtains and took in the picturesque morning. Then, she headed to the bathroom to take a shower and get cleaned up before she went downstairs for breakfast.

After she got out of the shower, Mindy wrapped her hair in a towel and rummaged through her suitcase in search of something to wear. Finally, she decided on a soft cotton V-neck t-shirt in black and a pair of light khaki shorts with a braided belt. The outfit was soft and comfortable, but dressy enough to be fashionable out on the town. With it, she fastened her modest silver cross necklace around her neck and held her long brown hair back in a hairclip. On her feet she had a pair of comfortable yet elegant black sandals. Slipping her cat's-eye glasses on to secure the final touch; Mindy looked over herself in the mirror, satisfied with her casual, classy look. Being a banker, she never left the house if she didn't look nice, but she was never obsessed with her appearance. Turning away, Mindy grabbed her tan purse and turned the lights off, closing the door behind her when she left her room.

The morning view of the terrace was beautiful, with the sun beaming in through the floor-to-ceiling glass windows. When Mindy stepped off the elevator and made her way to the continental breakfast room, she noticed that the tables were evenly spaced and there weren't too many people there. With the airy, open look and pleasant view, Mindy liked it immediately. Scanning the room, she chose a table close to the window and headed to the counter to get something to eat. Mindy was surprised that they had quite a selection. A maid in a blue uniform stood off to the side, helping people and supervising. True to her sparing appetite, Mindy picked a container of peach yogurt, a small bowl of cereal and a giant-size mug of steaming black coffee, Columbian roast.

With her tray filled, Mindy headed back over to the table by the window and sat down, picking up a Burlington newspaper to browse through while she ate. As she opened up her newspaper, Mindy took a long sip of her coffee, unfazed by the way the strong liquid burned her tongue. She was alternately eating and reading the newspaper when she was interrupted by a friendly voice.

"Good morning!" a deep male voice boomed, and Mindy looked up to see the friendly older businessman from the pool smiling down at her.

"Good morning," Mindy replied less boisterously, giving the man a smile.

"Beautiful day in Burlington, isn't it?" the man continued, looking appreciatively out the window at the scenery.

"Yes, definitely," Mindy agreed, finding the man to be an amiable companion. She motioned to the seat across from her. "Would you like to sit?"

The businessman dipped his head. "May I?" he asked. "I don't want to disturb your breakfast."

Mindy waved her hand. "No problem," she told him. "I don't know anyone here anyway, the company would be nice."

"Okay," he agreed, sitting down. "I don't know many folks either. My name is Ernest, by the way. Don't call me Ernie," he added with a laugh.

"Okay, *Ernest,*" Mindy replied. "I'm Mindy."

Mindy and Ernest chatted lightly over breakfast until Mindy stood up to go dump her tray. "I need to go, Ernest," she told him. "I want to look around the city and do some grocery shopping. It was nice talking to you."

"You too, Mindy," Ernest replied, looking up from his paper. "If you're looking for the market, there's one on Poplar Street, not too far from here."

"Thanks so much," Mindy replied, glad that she didn't have to try to find the grocery store.

Lifting her purse on her shoulder, Mindy left the breakfast room and walked through the lobby doors, bursting out into the beautiful summer morning. Closing her eyes, Mindy tilted her face up and took a deep breath of the fresh mountain air, tasting its crispness. Then, still smiling lightly, she made her way to her car and decided to get a move on with the shopping so that she would have time to leisurely explore the beautiful city. Getting in her car, she rolled the windows down and backed out of the parking lot, letting the fresh air stream in through her windows. There was a little more traffic on the main road that Mindy would have liked, but it was nothing like the congested snares that Mindy fought through every day in New Jersey. Following Ernest's directions, she found the drive to the market to be scenic and painless. The store itself was closer to the "suburbs" of the town, out of the downtown rush. Mindy parked in the parking lot and reached in her purse for the list she had made the night before.

It took Mindy quite a while to find everything she wanted in the store, since it was a much different layout from what she was used to. After she had gotten groceries, Mindy realized that she had to do some other errands such as go to the bank, find the laundromat, etc.

***

By the time Mindy finished all the things she had to do, it was almost 2:00 and she realized that she hadn't stopped for lunch. After Mindy put her groceries away, she decided that she'd rather go out to a restaurant or café than just sit in her room.

This time, Mindy took a more leisurely stroll around the city, taking time to look at the structure of the buildings and the amorphous shapes of the mountains in the distance. Amazed, Mindy looked around at the bustle of the city, feeling the energy of it. It was almost as if the city had a life of its own, Mindy thought, recalling the strange energy she felt the moment she laid eyes on it.

Smiling absently, Mindy bobbed her head to the rock music she was playing on her radio and drove down by the lake, slowing down to admire the quaint stores near the waterfront, but not yet finding a place that she wanted to stop for lunch.

Taking a right, Mindy found herself on a pretty, quiet street. The road itself had a steep incline, and both sides of the street were lined with trees and quaint old houses, late afternoon sunlight glimmering prettily through the blankets of leaves. Up at the top of the hill, Mindy took another right and found a small strip of shops that had a distant view of Lake Champlain. Among these quaint shops was a tall, dark brick building with a sign out front that read, *Manor House Coffee Shoppe.* As Mindy passed by it, she slowed down. This would be a perfect place to stop for lunch, Mindy thought, as the quaint coffee shop seemed to call to her from across the street. Having made up her mind, Mindy parked on the street across from the building and paid the parking meter, closing her car door behind her. As she headed across the street, she became aware of the lightest sense of tingling energy that surrounded the place, the same that she had felt the first night in her hotel room. Since the feeling was pleasant, Mindy continued on. When she reached the glass door and stepped in, she was surrounded by a wave ten times stronger, getting the sensation that she was in the heart of the city itself.

Looking around, Mindy thought that it was the most beautiful coffee shop she had ever been in. There weren't many coffee shops near her apartment in New Jersey, and that was a disappointment, because Mindy loved coffee shops. But as she let the door close behind her, Mindy took a few minutes to really study the place.

The architecture of the old house was beautiful, with crown molding and dark mahogany wood, and a wide arched doorway into another sitting room. Straight ahead was the counter, with a board above it detailing all of the available coffee flavors in different colors. Under the counter was a glass case loaded with delicious-looking baked goods of all kinds: pies, cakes, cookies, scones, and more. Though the color scheme was dark, the place was ultimately cheerful, with bouquets of flowers on every table, paintings on the walls, and ceiling fans mounted on the high ceiling.

Since it was still lunch hour, the place was moderately busy and there was a slight line, but Mindy didn't mind. The view down the hill was picturesque, the colorful sailboats on Lake Champlain visible in the distance.

When Mindy reached the counter, she ordered a large cinnamon latte with extra whipped cream and a piece of brown sugar-pecan coffee cake. The barista, a hip-looking blond college guy, smiled at Mindy and named the price. She smiled back and handed him her credit card. He swiped it and handed it back to her, followed by the cake and coffee. She thanked him and he wished her a good day.

Looking around, Mindy decided to sit in the main room by the window, looking out over the lake. Stopping at the napkin counter, she picked out silverware and napkins and proceeded to a cozy two-top by the window.

With a pleasant sigh, Mindy sat down next to the open window and let the breeze cool her scalding coffee. *What a beautiful place,* she thought as she carefully sipped the sweet liquid. Never in her life had she felt so relaxed, so content. Leaning back, she stretched and unclipped her hair, running her hands through the damp waves before replacing her hairclip.

As she sipped her coffee, Mindy gazed out the window and enjoyed the scenery, contemplating how the city seemed to glimmer all the way down the hill, sunlight reflecting golden waves off of everything. But here at the top of the hill the force seemed to come straight from the sun, as if this was the most magical place in the city. Idly, Mindy picked up a magazine that someone had left on the chair and flipped through it indifferently.

Taking another sip of her coffee, Mindy decided that it was still searing-hot and could use a little bit more cream. Leaving her purse on her chair, Mindy got up and went to the table with cream and napkins, carefully taking the lid off of her cup and stirring in a little bit more cream.

After she stirred in the cream, Mindy lifted the cup to her lips and took a small sip. *Much better,* she thought. The coffee was still pleasantly hot but it didn't burn her tongue quite so severely. Swallowing appreciatively, Mindy turned to go back to her table, glancing up at the menu board one more time as she walked. But as she looked over, she was suddenly so overcome with sensation that she nearly choked on her coffee, spilling a thin line of it down her shirt. For behind the counter had appeared the most fascinating man she had ever seen.

The guy seemed to be around Mindy's age, give or take a year or two, but his face appeared wiser than his years. He was lean but fit; she could see his muscles as he lifted a heavy pitcher from behind the counter and poured a cup of water for the next woman in line. He had soft, side-swept brown hair, long-lashed eyes so pale blue-gray that they were almost colorless, and brown tortoise-shell glasses. As Mindy watched him, she noticed that he looked cool and comfortable in his black barista apron, and he appeared very soft spoken but smiled at all of his customers. Mindy felt an additional thrill run through her when she noticed the ornate blue dragon tattoo winding around his upper arm.

For the longest time, all Mindy could do was stand there and stare at him as he ran the espresso machine while talking to one of the customers. Finally, when she could tear herself away, Mindy went to sit down at her table, suddenly feeling the urge to finish her coffee so she could go back up and get another one.

Mindy sipped the rest of her drink, still intermittently studying the charismatic guy behind the counter. It was more than his looks that made him attractive, Mindy mused. It was his whole being, his presence. The effect when she had first laid eyes on him had been so electrifying, almost like being surrounded in a powerful force field. Tipping her cup back, Mindy finished her drink and rose to go get her second cup, a knot of anxious anticipation settling in her stomach. How was she supposed to go and talk to this man when she couldn't even look at him without choking on her coffee?

Making sure she didn't have a mouthful of coffee this time, Mindy brushed a hand through her hair, gracefully setting her shoulders back as she glided toward the end of the line.

One or two people ordered before her, but suddenly, Mindy was thrust to the front of the line and found herself face-to-face with her mystery man.

"What can I do for you?" he asked in a pleasant, friendly tone.

The moment she locked eyes with him, Mindy was paralyzed. She gazed into his face and noticed that his pale eyes seemed to be dancing with flecks of sunshine, and his faint smile was pure and sincere.

"Holy Lord," Mindy breathed involuntarily. Being this close to him was downright lethal. Her entire body hummed as she was filled with the essence of his presence. Remembering herself, Mindy cleared her throat. "One medium black coffee, please," she finally managed. "I'd like Columbian."

The man didn't seem to be disturbed or make fun of her for her lapse in speech. Instead, he just smiled again. "Good choice," he told her with a light wink. "That will be one-ninety seven."

With clumsy fingers, Mindy withdrew her credit card from her purse and handed it to him. All too soon, her coffee was done and he handed it to her, sending another spark raging through her veins when their fingers brushed.

"Thank you," Mindy managed, flashing him a demure, flirtatious smile.

He returned her smile and wished her a good day, his eyes still lingering on hers.

Balancing her drink in her hand, Mindy let the heels of her sandals clack seductively on the dark-tiled floor. Even from the back, she could feel the searing heat of his gaze still lingering on her, caressing her hips, trailing down her legs. Mindy was used to being stared at, but being under the scrutiny of the mysterious barista was an entirely different sensation, searing hot and delightful. With her heart pounding, Mindy decided to have a bit of fun. She arched her back and ran a hand through her hair, wanting to keep the man's gaze on her as she disappeared into the crowd.

Suddenly, Mindy's sexy, strappy sandals hit a slippery patch on the floor, and before she knew it, she was airborne, a stream of Columbian coffee shooting straight into the air. As fast as she was in the air, flying, Mindy hit the ground hard and fell flat on her back as a deluge of coffee splattered down beside her, some of it soaking her shirt.

It took Mindy a moment to regain her bearings as she was lying on the floor, wincing in agony. Slowly, she became aware of the swarm of raised voices around her and several people pointing, staring. "Damn," she groaned irritably, trying to push herself up off the floor with some dignity.

"Careful," a quiet voice spoke above her and Mindy looked up to see the kind face of her mystery man above her. He offered her a hand and helped her ever so gently to her feet. His grip was warm and strong but his hand on her back was gentle.

Once Mindy was on her feet, she looked around at the crowd that had gathered and felt a wave of mortification wash over her.

The mystery man must have felt her discomfort, because he waved his hand at the people. "All right, folks, we'll be fine," he reassured them in his soft tone of voice, firmly letting them know that the show was over. He locked eyes with a blonde girl with a mop and she flashed him the sign that she'd handle it. Nodding in thanks, he started to escort Mindy outside for some fresh air.

Embarrassed, Mindy realized that she was still in his arms and tried to detach herself, but she tripped over her own feet, forcing him to catch her again. "I'm so sorry," Mindy muttered, her face crimson as he led her outside. "I mean…"

"It's fine," he cut her off softly, maintaining his firm but gentle grip on her shoulders. For a moment, Mindy lost herself in the heat of his arm across her shoulders, wishing she could stay in his arms forever.

But before she knew it, her mystery man was gently setting her down at an outside table.

Pulling out his chair, he sat across from her. "Are you okay?" he asked, looking deeply into her eyes. "I won't leave until you are."

Mindy sighed and nodded. "I will be," she responded with a mirthless laugh. "Just a bit bruised and embarrassed, that's all."

The guy grinned. "Well, I hope you feel better soon," he answered sincerely. "The way you threw that coffee was pretty impressive, though, I've never seen anything like it before."

At first, Mindy was insulted, but when she looked up at him, his pale eyes were twinkling with kindness. Realizing that he wasn't making fun of her, Mindy began to laugh. "I have to admit," she agreed. "I've never done that before."

The guy was still smiling, and then he gave her a curious sideways look. "You're new to town," he remarked softly, his eyes searching hers.

Mindy barked out a short laugh. "That obvious, huh?" she chuckled. Looking up, she smiled at him. "I'm Araminta Cullen. I just got here yesterday, and it is the most beautiful place I have ever been. Burlington is paradise, especially this coffee shop."

The guy shrugged modestly and coloured slightly. "I'm so glad you like it," he replied, shaking her hand lightly. "Welcome, Araminta."

"You can call me…" Mindy started to say, but then she decided the loved the sound of her full name on his lips.

"Pardon?" he asked.

Mindy shook her head. "Never mind," she told him. "I can't thank you enough for rescuing me."

He looked on her with kind eyes and a boyish smile. "It's no problem, I'm glad I could help," he replied modestly. Then, he gave her an apologetic grin. "I'm afraid I need to get back to work," he said softly, rising from his chair. "The drive-thru is inundated. But it was a pure pleasure to meet you, Araminta. I hope to see you again."

Mindy rose from her chair as well, deciding to go back to the hotel and change out of her coffee-soaked shirt. "You, too," she whispered after him as he disappeared back into the café with a friendly wave. As she got in her car to drive back to the hotel, she realized that she didn't even know his name.

Chapter Seven

Later that afternoon, when Mindy got back to her hotel, she changed out of her coffee-stained clothes and stuffed them in a laundry bag, slightly disappointed that one of her favorite shirts had been ruined. *Oh, well,* she thought. *At least it's black and won't show.* Looking out the window of her hotel room, Mindy glanced at the sun, which was prominently set in the western sky, signaling the end of the day was near. Grimacing, Mindy rubbed her sore back and decided that she wanted to go for a swim and soak in the hot tub. Glad that she finally had a plan, Mindy put on her ruffled black bathing suit, twisted her hair up in a bun, and wrapped herself in a towel to head down to the pool room.

When she got into the pool room, Mindy was relieved to see that she had the place to herself. Feeling chilled from the constant air conditioning in her room, Mindy set her things down on the chair and dipped into the hot tub, sighing with pleasure as she sank beneath the warm water. The heat did wonders for her sore back muscles, and she stretched out and relaxed. As she lounged in the pleasant, bubbling water, Mindy tilted her neck from side to side and went over in her mind all that had happened that day. *Holy hell, could I have made a bigger fool of myself?* She thought, shaking her head as she recalled the coffee shop scene. Ever since she had arrived in Burlington, things had changed, she realized. Back in New Jersey, she was focused completely on her work and gave the cold shoulder to any man who approached her. She just didn't date. It was simple, and it worked.

Thinking about this, Mindy frowned. What was the deal with the guy in the coffee shop, she wondered. Why was she so immediately attracted to him? It hadn't been since she was seventeen that those types of feelings had emerged, and she was terrified. Uneasily, Mindy shifted in the water and thought that she couldn't have possibly botched the situation any worse. She had been trying to make a good impression, but instead, she had wiped out completely in the middle of the room, caused a huge spectacle, and had to be picked up off of the floor by the guy she was trying to impress. *That is precisely why I don't date,* she thought with a mirthless smile. *It never ends well.*

Once she was over the anxiety of all of it, Mindy found herself thinking about the mysterious man himself. Who was he, she wondered, disappointed that she hadn't even gotten his name. And more importantly, what was it about him that captured the attentions of Araminta the Ice Queen? Thinking about him, Mindy smiled fondly. He was so kind and attentive, not making fun of her when she slipped, and his eyes were so wise. Was he just doing his job? Or was the sincerity in his eyes more than mere professionalism?

Yawning, Mindy realized that it had been a tiring day. At least she had gotten some errands done and had time to enjoy herself too. Looking up at the wall-mounted clock, she decided that she had had enough of the hot tub and wanted to swim in the regular pool for a while.

Startled by the cooler water, it took Mindy a few minutes to adjust to the contrast, but she enjoyed it after the hot tub had started to get too hot. Mindy had never been much of a swimmer, but she enjoyed the feeling of being able to float weightlessly in the water. She only stayed in the pool for maybe twenty more minutes before she decided to get out and go clean up for the evening. Wrapping herself in her towel, she left the room and went back to the elevators, her shoes squeaking on the floor again. As she passed the fitness room, Mindy gave it a rueful glance. *Shoot*, she thought, realizing with a frown that she hadn't worked out that morning. Taking a deep breath, Mindy tried to tell herself that she was on vacation, not to worry about it.

When Mindy got back to her room, she turned up the air and took a shower yet again to rinse the chlorine off of her. When she got out, she was glad to be done showering, and dressed in a baggy, comfortable t-shirt and pair of shorts. Briefly, she debated about whether she wanted to go out for dinner, but then she decided that she was still tired from the trip, and from the busy day she had had. Besides, it was late, and she didn't want to try to find a restaurant. Comfortable with her decision, she went to the kitchenette and heated up a pan of soup and brewed a pot of black coffee.

Later, when Mindy was reading before bed, she sat in the silence of her hotel room and began to think of all the things that were troubling her, feeling like she was being pulled back into the mire of the life she had left behind in New Jersey. It was like the more she tried to forget about it, the harder it surged up in her memory. Frowning, she set down the book that she was attempting to read and clicked on the radio for some background noise to distract her. When she turned the radio on, she searched until she found an 80's alt-rock station, which was playing one of her favorite rock and roll songs. Rising from her bed and shutting off the light, Mindy found herself drawn to the window. Gently, she parted the curtains, but nothing prepared her for the spectacular view.

Awestruck, Mindy gazed out through the glass, mesmerized by the night lights of the sparkling city. Colorful signs and twinkling lights glowed in the distance of the downtown, but the hotel courtyard was quiet with only small lamps lighting the walking path. Up above, a full moon shone down on the garden, and Mindy could faintly see how the light reflected on the flowers, illuminating their pale pink hue. As she stood there, the rock and roll song ended and a slower ballad came on. Mindy was amazed by the sensation; the city was pulsating with an overload of energy, but it was controlled, seeming to rise and fall with the sensuous beat of the song. It had been said that every city had a heartbeat, but it wasn't until she got to Burlington that Mindy really believed in it. Taking a deep breath, Mindy let herself relax and leaned on the windowsill, still gazing out, watching the city.

In her dreamy state, Mindy once again began to think about the mysterious man in the coffee shop. Though their first meeting had been somewhat of a chaotic incident, the man himself had been so calm, so kind. Thinking about him more deeply, Mindy realized that she had never in her life met a man like him who seemed so free from the snares of humanity. Even though she had only talked to him for a few minutes, his presence was magical to her and she positively longed to see him again.

Feeling much better, Mindy spun away from the window and paraded across her bedroom, dancing to the music. She felt slightly foolish for dancing with herself, but soon she got over it and danced until she collapsed into her bed and drifted to sleep.

Chapter Eight

The next morning, Mindy rolled over and blinked herself awake shortly before 7AM. When she finally opened her gray eyes, she was greeted once again by the wonderful sight of the sun streaming in through the curtains. Running a hand through her hair, she checked the clock and decided to get up, feeling refreshed and well-rested. Yawning serenely, she leaned back and stretched before swinging her feet over the side of the bed and making her way to the bathroom. Meeting her own eyes in the mirror, Mindy decided to hit the fitness room for an hour or two before starting her day.

In the bathroom, Mindy only did the bare minimum: brushed her teeth, washed her face, and put on some deodorant before she changed into her sports clothes. Once she had her gray t-shirt and black shorts on, Mindy twisted her hair into a bun to keep it out of her way and laced up her sneakers. Before she left the room, she grabbed her music player and swigged two glasses of her signature exercise cocktail: orange juice, electrolyte-rich mineral water, and a touch of lime extract. It was certainly an unusual taste, but Mindy choked it down briefly before wiping her mouth on her sleeve and stuffing her room key into her pocket. Flicking the lights off, she left the room and made sure that the door was locked behind her.

After she got off of the elevator, Mindy looked around at the cheerful, sunlit lobby and took a moment to appreciate the beautiful morning as she walked along the terrace to the fitness room. Pulling her key back out of her pocket, Mindy swiped it along the door to let herself into the exercise room. Once she stepped in, Mindy was glad to see that she had the place to herself. With no time to waste, Mindy plugged her headphones into her music player, and started to warm up, bobbing her head to the beat-heavy dance music that came on.

When she had gone through her warm-up aerobics, Mindy hopped onto a treadmill and began her run, turning up her music until it was blasting in her ears. Back in New Jersey, Mindy had never really enjoyed her exercise routine; it was just another compulsion to fill her time. But here, as she ran, she felt alive, conscious of the pounding of her feet on the rubber and the burning of the breath in her lungs as her favorite hard-rock band raged their way through one of their famous head-banging tracks. She was so absorbed in her workout that she failed to notice two heavyset men come in and begin lifting weights in the corner.

Finally, after running three miles, Mindy slowed to a walk and stepped off of the treadmill, splashing her face with water and taking a long swig from her canteen. "Nice run, little lady," one of the men piped up from the corner, his eyes roaming over Mindy's slim figure as he continued to lift the barbell up and down. "You in the Olympics?"

Mindy shook her head and wiped her face on her sleeve in a very unladylike manner. "Nope, not me," she answered with a shrug as she wiped down her equipment. Without further conversation, Mindy left the room and headed back to her hotel room.

After her run, Mindy peeled off her sweaty clothes and hopped immediately into the shower, grateful for the cold spray on her flushed face.

When she had finished washing herself off, Mindy shut off the shower and dried her face on her towel, fluffing it in her hair before she headed back into her bedroom to get dressed. Opening her suitcase, Mindy decided that she would like to go out for breakfast as opposed to sitting in the nice but dull dining hall downstairs. In fact, she thought, she would like to go try her hand at the Manor House again. With this thought, a jolt of thrilling uncertainty shot through her, but she continued. Finally, with a faint smile touching the corners of her lips, she lifted out a lacy pale-pink tank top and a pair of cropped camo shorts. Yes, this was it. When Mindy had donned her clothes, she looked in the mirror and her approval was confirmed. The lacy tank top was sweet and flirty, skimming over her ultra-slim figure, showing just enough of her meager cleavage. The shorts cupped her hips and showed off her long, slim legs. With a grim chuckle, Mindy decided that she had better wear sneakers so that she didn't repeat yesterday's mortifying wipeout. Besides, the sneakers represented Mindy's down-to-earth stability, in the psychic-symbolic sense.

After she was dressed, Mindy brushed her damp hair and loosely twisted it back in a hairclip with dangling strands framing her face. Setting her glasses on the bridge of her nose, Mindy fastened her sterling-silver cross necklace around her neck and rubbed down her arms with rose-scented body lotion. Satisfied with her appearance, feeling cool and comfortable, Mindy grabbed her practical tan purse and flicked the lights out, once again leaving her hotel room.

Outside, Mindy was greeted with a breath of sweet, fresh mountain air, and she inhaled deeply, sighing with contentment. The sun was shining down from a cloudless sky, glimmering off of the trees and buildings, a gentle breeze ruffled the dark-green leaves on the surrounding trees and in the distance, the mysterious bluish-green mountains seemed to go on endlessly. *It's so beautiful here,* Mindy thought. *Just like heaven.* With that thought, Mindy walked to her car and aimed the remote keys at it from afar. Then, she climbed into the driver's seat, turned on the max AC, and cranked up the radio.

As Mindy made her way towards the Manor House, she was both extremely nervous and zinging with anticipation. As she continued driving, questions relentlessly peppered her mind. Would he be there? Would he be happy to see her? Did he think she was an idiot? Did he remember her name? The list went on and on. But when Mindy began ascending the hill toward the café, she felt the same tingling energy that she had sensed the day before. It seemed that the life force of the city was stronger near the top of the hill. When Mindy parked in the lot, she was disappointed to see that the café was pretty busy. *A lot of people must stop here for breakfast,* she figured.

Stepping inside, Mindy was pleasantly surprised to see that it wasn't as busy as it looked. Several people were sitting silently at their tables, reading or studying. Others were having hushed conversations, and some of them were just getting takeout. Surveying the room, Mindy studied her surroundings, enjoying the pretty morning in the old house. Suddenly, her gaze locked onto her mystery man and a bolt of raw energy shot through her, threatening to knock her over. Stumbling to regain her balance, Mindy gazed at him, even more aware in the morning light of how beautiful he was. He was sitting at a table near the window, looking out over the lake and sipping from a steaming mug of black coffee. On his plate he had half of a breakfast roll, and a thick paperback lay on the table next to him. Mesmerized, Mindy watched as he bobbed his head to the groovy lounge music coming from the speakers above, seeming to just flow with the beat.

"Excuse me, Miss, are you in line?" Mindy's thoughts were interrupted by the sound of a voice behind her. Turning

51

around, she saw an older gentleman giving her a quizzical stare.

"Yes, I am," Mindy answered quickly, tearing her gaze off of her mystery man and moving ahead in line.

When she got up to the counter, Mindy wasn't sure what she wanted. Everything looked so good, and the air was thick with the aroma of fresh baked goods and rich coffee. Taking an appreciative sniff, Mindy scanned the menu and decided to try a medium cinnamon latte and a blueberry bagel with cream cheese. The lady in front of her paid and left, and Mindy was up, face-to-face with a heavyset, harassed-looking girl.

"Can I help you?" she asked tiredly.

Mindy recited her order and paid with her credit card, conscious of the girl's curious stare. With a grimace, Mindy realized that that girl had been there for the Great Wipeout. Not giving a dime about what this person thought, Mindy took her coffee and bagel and turned around to go find a seat. As she collected a napkin and fork, Mindy was drawn once again to her mysterious man, feeling a twinge of nervousness as she headed toward him.

Trying to be as calm and cool as possible, Mindy made her way across the floor, light in her sneaker-clad steps. She was aware that her heart was pounding and her hands were shaking as she neared the table where he was sitting and reading. *Onestep…twostep…threestep…* Mindy recited to herself, willing her feet not to slip on the floor again.

"Good morning, Araminta," the soft, husky voice broke her trance, and Mindy looked over to see the mystery man looking up from his novel and smiling merrily at her.

Relieved, Mindy stopped counting and a scarlet flush swept over her face. "Good morning," she answered cheerfully, breaking into a beaming smile. "I didn't think you'd remember my name."

"Of course I did," he gave her a sunny smile and a modest shrug. "I remember you quite well."

Mindy coloured again. "Yeah, that was a pretty unforgettable fall," she admitted ruefully. Looking down, she searched his face for impatience or disinterest, but his pale gray eyes were sparkling. "Do you mind if I sit with you?"

"Not at all," he answered with a friendly gesture toward the chair across the table. Smiling, Mindy sank down into the seat and sipped her latte.

"This is delicious," she remarked. "Definitely my favorite coffee shop."

The mystery man looked pleased. "I'm glad," he replied. "I love this place."

Curiously, Mindy studied him as he took another sip of his black coffee. "I never got to ask you yesterday, and I've been wondering… what's your name?"

He smiled. "Well, everyone calls me B.," he responded cheerfully, swallowing his coffee and wiping his mouth on a napkin.

Mindy was intrigued by his strange answer. "What is B. short for?" she wondered, looking out the window at the beautiful sunny morning.

She turned to B, who shrugged. "I'm just B.," he answered. "B. Fairmont."

"Ah," Mindy sipped her coffee and extended her hand. "It's a pleasure to meet you, B."

B. clasped Mindy's hand, sending a trail of gentle sparks shooting up her arm. His hand was warm and callused, soft to the touch but clearly work-worn. "The pleasure is mine," he said quietly, and Mindy felt a stirring of heat in her long-dormant core as she imagined his wry mouth on hers, those golden hands streaking down her sides to cup her hips, she would run her fingers through his hair as he pulled her closer….

With an embarrassed laugh, Mindy cleared her throat and released his hand. "Sorry, I was just thinking," she babbled, her face flushing a deeper shade of crimson.

"That's okay," his eyes twinkled and he gave her an amused grin, which just caused her to turn red again. Once she was settled down, Mindy took another sip of her coffee and sighed, still smiling at her own foolishness. Looking up, she saw that B. was still smiling faintly as well.

"Tell me about yourself," the request tumbled out of Mindy's mouth as an impetuous plea as she scanned his appearance-- softly feathered brown hair, long-lashed, pale blue-gray eyes, black t-shirt that revealed his blue dragon tattoo winding around his muscular bicep. "Are you a college student?"

B. seemed to be pleased by her interest, and slightly amused. "Nope, I'm a landlord," he replied.

Mindy was both surprised and impressed. "That's very cool," she told him, brushing a wisp of hair from her face. "But why do you work in a coffee shop?"

"I own it," he responded, a gleam of pride misting over his eyes. "I built this place with my own hands."

"That's so wonderful," Mindy breathed. "This is a magical place." She barely refrained from saying *you're magical.*

B. coloured visibly at her praise, which Mindy thought just added to his charm. Beautiful, hardworking, sensitive, modest landlord? Amazing. "So what about you, Araminta?" he wondered. "What do you do?"

"I'm a banker," she answered. "Well, technically, I'm the head of the Real Estate department at the Newark branch of Colony Bank."

B. looked intrigued. "Wow, that's pretty cool," he observed with a smile. "You do seem to have a banker's straightforward way about you."

"Yeah," Mindy agreed cheerfully, blushing as she sipped her latte. "My job is all in black and white, I guess I have to be straightforward."

They talked some more, and Mindy found that B. was richly knowledgeable on a plethora of topics, and she learned so much that her head was starting to spin. He seemed particularly versed in Burlington and Vermont history, often adopting a faraway look in his eyes when he told her vibrant stories of the city's past.

"So, have you lived here all of your life?" Mindy asked him, yearning to find out more about this beautiful man who beguiled her so.

He sipped his coffee thoughtfully. "I have," he replied, an unreadable expression flickering in his gray eyes. "What about you, where are you from?"

Mindy was surprised by his flippant answer and abrupt subject change, curious as to why he didn't elaborate. She was silent for several moments but decided not to push the issue, especially since they had just met. "I was born in the mountains of Montana," she said quietly. "But I never got to see it. My family moved to New Jersey when I was just a baby and I've lived there for twenty-six years. But the only place I've ever felt at home is here."

B. was also silent for several moments, and slowly, the guarded look faded from his eyes and they were filled with bittersweet warmth. Mindy couldn't explain why she suddenly felt choked up, but she blinked and wiped her eyes with her napkin, amazed and disturbed by the great waves of emotion she felt radiating between her and the handsome, mysterious stranger. After only a brief moment, B.'s gaze returned to normal and he shrugged. "I'm glad you like it here," he told her in a lighter tone. "It's a cool town."

Checking her watch, Mindy didn't realize that she had been sitting and talking to B. for almost two hours.

"Goodness, I'm so sorry," Mindy apologized with a short laugh. "I didn't mean to sit and pester you for so long."

B. smiled at her and leaned back in his chair. "Cut it out, Araminta," he teased softly, flicking a straw wrapper at her. "I enjoyed your company very much."

Mindy's heart rate sped up and she swallowed hard. Was B. flirting with her? He enjoyed her company? Blushing deeply, Mindy grinned and flicked the straw wrapper back at him, eliciting a chuckle from him. "Well, I want to thank you for talking to me, and your coffee shop is definitely the best in town," she told him. "I'll definitely be back."

B. smiled modestly. "Thanks," he said almost shyly. "And you, too. Anytime you want, just stop in. I'm almost always here."

"For sure," Mindy answered.

Just then, they were interrupted by a skinny, black-haired guy in an apron who rushed up to the table. "Hey, B., the kitchen sink's messed up. Water is threatening to go everywhere!" he exclaimed urgently, waving his hands.

"Alright, I'm on it," B. answered abruptly, rising from his chair with efficient determination and walking toward the kitchen in long strides. Mindy sat back and enjoyed the view of his muscular back and lean backside as he walked away.

Discreetly, Mindy rose from the table and hung back near the trash can, craning her neck to see into the kitchen without being obviously noticed. She saw B. carrying in a bucket and setting down on the floor. Looking at the sink, Mindy could see that it was indeed almost overflowing. She watched B. say something tersely to the skinny guy, who was just waving his hands and talking loudly. With a grimace, B. opened the lower cabinets, pulled on a pair of rubber gloves, and began to tinker with the pipes. With a powerful twist of his arms and a loud *thwunk,* B. turned the wrench and the water began draining from the sink. Amidst the melee in the kitchen, she heard him explaining something about the stopper being jammed, an obvious explanation. She watched as he talked down the antic chef, who nodded and dropped his hands to his sides. After he carried the tool bucket away, he blew out a breath as everything returned to normal. Briefly, he rinsed his hands in the tap and turned to head back out to his table.

Before he could see her loitering like a fool, Mindy turned and attempted to bolt back to the table, briefly tripping over a table leg before she sat back down. When he came back, she asked him innocently what had happened, not wanting him to know that she had been gawking at him while he worked.

He explained it to her, seemingly cheerful about the whole matter, and she was impressed by his strength and knowledge. "Hey, I should go help the staff with the lunch hour rush," he explained apologetically, gesturing to the clock. "They're gonna start arriving any minute."

"I bet," Mindy answered understandingly, rising from the table and collecting her garbage. She flashed him a beaming smile. "Hey, I'll see you later; I'm going to explore the city."

"Well, enjoy yourself, Araminta," B. told her, waving and grinning briefly before he disappeared into the back.

Chapter Nine

After the pleasant morning at the Manor House, Mindy decided to look around the city and do some shopping along the Church Street Marketplace. The pedestrian cobblestone street was a well-known attraction in Burlington, and she had read about it in a tourist magazine she had picked up. Generally, Mindy wasn't a big shopper, but mainly because she just didn't have time. But here on vacation, she thought it would be cool to explore the quaint boutiques.

Still smiling faintly from her encounter with B., Mindy climbed into her car and backed slowly out of her parking space, checking in her rearview mirror for oncoming traffic. Shading her eyes from the sun, Mindy turned the car around and cranked up the radio again, heading down the hilly street the same way she came. *God, what a beautiful day,* Mindy thought to herself while she bobbed her head to the music, drumming her fingers on the steering wheel. So far the day was just about perfect: brilliant sunshine covering the entire city with a golden glow, sky blue and clear with just the barest wisp of clouds, noble old trees standing tall, the sunlight shimmering through their leaves. And from the top of the hill, Lake Champlain was visible, the water a deep, dusky blue with the white outlines of sailboats floating along serenely. To the right and left of the street, people walked in summer clothing, laughing and talking.

As she continued, Mindy found herself once again thinking of B. Honestly, Mindy was pleasantly surprised by how well the meeting went. Not only had he remembered her name and not thought she was an idiot, but they ended up talking all morning. Seeing him did nothing to satisfy the longing in Mindy's heart, for all she wanted was to see him again. There was just an instant connection, something sacred and undeniable.

When Mindy left the hill street, she turned and made her way through the slightly congested center of town, looking for the Church Street Marketplace. A sign indicated that it was ahead, and Mindy pulled into a parking lot and got a ticket from the meter.

Brushing a stray wisp of hair from her face, Mindy adjusted her sunglasses and lifted her purse on her shoulder, taking an appreciative look around at the pretty little town. Ready to start her shopping extravaganza, Mindy crossed the street and followed the easygoing flow of pedestrian traffic down the hill, taking time to admire the quaint cafés and boutiques that lined the streets.

When she reached Church Street, Mindy took a look around and entered the cobblestone street, following the relaxed crowd meandering through the shops. A few shops, Mindy passed because she had no interest. Seeing a bookstore ahead, she stopped and figured that she could find some new reads while she was on her vacation. The mid-afternoon sun was warm as it beat down on the street, and Mindy began to feel slightly overheated. Wanting some peace and cooler climate, she entered the bookstore and was refreshed by a much-needed icy blast of air conditioning. Sighing with relief, Mindy tucked her sunglasses into her purse and took out her reading glasses. The lady at the counter looked up and gave Mindy a friendly greeting, which she returned. As she shopped, Mindy mused that she hadn't done much reading for quite some time. It wasn't because she didn't like it, Mindy loved to read. She just didn't always have a lot of time or energy to do anything back home.

Browsing the shelves, Mindy searched for a book that would catch her fancy. Up on the top shelf, she picked up a white book with red letters and read the synopsis, intrigued and impressed. The story was about a young therapist who ran a successful, compassionate support group for criminals, but her personal life was falling apart. Mindy loved psychological memoirs, so she decided to definitely get it. Another book, a purple novel, was a sensual story of a red-hot duke and his feisty mistress, amidst the deep propriety of Victorian society. Enjoying herself, Mindy picked out several more interesting choices before she proceeded to the checkout counter with five new books.

Up at the counter, Mindy set her purchases down and the woman began scanning them through, making pleasant small talk as she typed in the bar codes.

"Are you from here?" the woman asked Mindy with a smile.

"I'm on vacation," Mindy answered. "But I feel more at home here than anywhere else."

The woman smiled wistfully. "Burlington does that to you," she commented. "Once you get here, you never want to leave."

The two of them talked for several minutes about the weather and the books, before the woman bagged Mindy's books and wished her a good day. Thanking her, Mindy took her bag and slipped her sunglasses back down over her face, stepping out once again into the blazing sun.

Looking around, Mindy ventured into many shops and explored, not buying a whole lot more. Shortly after she came out of a scented candle store, she went into the next one, which sold clothes, shoes, and jewelry. Curious, Mindy wandered in and decided she could use some new clothes. But to her disappointment, much of the merchandise was overpriced and not to her liking. Turning away from the clothing rack, she went to look at the shoes. Mindy always liked to shop for shoes; they were her favorite, although all the shoes she bought were black, brown, flat, and practical. The fanciest pairs of shoes she owned were the conservative black pumps that she wore to work, and maybe the sandals she had slipped in at the Manor House. Since Mindy wasn't known to be a fanciful girl, she tended to stick to the basics and cut time, always cramming in as much work as possible. But as she looked at the shoe rack, Mindy saw several pairs of beautiful shoes, and she longed to try them on. The afternoon sun slanted in the window, illuminating a pair of dainty silver sandals with a 1-inch heel. With a wistful sigh, Mindy picked them up and looked them over, falling in love with them immediately. *I wish I had somewhere to wear these,* Mindy thought sadly to herself. She never went anywhere that would warrant something so fancy. Turning them over in her hands, Mindy was lost deep in thought when a voice behind her interrupted her.

"That is a beautiful pair of shoes," a female voice said behind her. "I'd get them, because you will never find shoes like that again."

Puzzled, Mindy turned around and saw a tall, lithe, black-haired woman a little older than her smiling at her. The woman's hair was pulled back in a swingy ponytail, slightly shorter than Mindy's. Her eyes were bright and almond-shaped behind her black glasses, matching her olive skin tone. She wore a V-neck jade-green T-shirt and a pair of extremely short black shorts adorned with white skull-and-crossbones. In her hands, she carried a pair of red stiletto heels that matched her long red fingernails. "I really like these, but I have nowhere to wear them," Mindy explained, barking out a short laugh. "It just makes me think of the social life I *don't* have."

The woman shook her head. "Dude, my boyfriend dumped me three months ago and I'm still getting over it." She held up the scarlet-red stilettos and grinned. "The fruits of capitalism are temptingly therapeutic."

With a smile, Mindy relented. "All right, you convinced me," she laughed as she picked up her silver sandals, deciding that she really liked this woman. "Thanks, I really wanted these."

The lady shrugged. "No problem," she answered and extended her hand, which was covered with stacks of jangly bangles. "I'm Belinda."

Smiling, Mindy shook Belinda's hand. "Nice to meet you," she replied. "I'm Mindy."

As they continued shopping, the two women continued talking, and Mindy found Belinda to be a very interesting person. She was lively and engaging, candid and intelligent. "So, what do you do for a living?" Mindy asked, curious as to where this eccentric woman fit in.

"I'm a dean at the university," Belinda explained. "Though you probably couldn't tell by looking at me."

Mindy smiled. "That's really cool," she answered. Looking down, Mindy noticed that Belinda had a bookstore bag too. "I take it you like to read?"

"I do," Belinda responded with a smile. "I love reading, shoe shopping, and wild sex in equal measure."

Amused by Belinda's dry wit, Mindy busted out laughing. "Yeah," she agreed, blushing when she thought of B. "That would certainly be nice."

The women shopped together for a while longer, until Belinda checked her watch and said she had to go to the office for a minute. "It was great to meet you, Mindy," she told her. "We'll have to talk again. Want to hang out tonight?"

"Absolutely," Mindy replied, grateful for the invitation. "I barely know anyone in this city."

"Okay, cool," Belinda sounded excited. "Here's my number. We can meet at the Redwood Lounge around seven if you want. It's a great place, just around the corner from here. The food is amazing and you can maybe meet some of the ladies at the U. We're there a lot."

"Awesome," Mindy answered. "I'll see you later."

***

Back in her hotel room, Mindy had finished shopping and was looking through the things she had bought. Her five new books looked very entertaining, and with some persuasion from Belinda, she had bought a few pairs of fancy shoes and some sexy underwear. "You never know when you're gonna need that," Belinda had told her with a wise look in her eye. "Trust me."

With a chuckle, Mindy nodded to herself, realizing how right Belinda was. Even though she had only spent an hour or two with the woman, she knew that they would get along great. Belinda was wild and wacky in contrast to Mindy's calm practicality, but she was also wise and compassionate, gently helping Mindy step up when she couldn't. Mindy had a special talent, an intuition even, of what people were like, and she had clicked with Belinda immediately. The only two people she had ever liked immediately like that were B. and Belinda.

Distracted by the sad ballad flowing from the speakers of the radio, Mindy was momentarily swept into the dark memories of her past. Love had never gone well for her, she knew that much. Her parents were average middle-class professionals, and everything had gone well until her parents got divorced when she was ten. It was an ugly, messy split, and her mother ended up making false claims against her father, earning full custody of their only daughter. Aaron Cullen had disappeared back into the mountains of Montana where he was from, and Mindy's mother, Elaine Sutherland, stayed in New Jersey, her hometown. After that, Mindy remembered, life became hell. Her mother was shrill and overbearing, hovering over Mindy's every move. She was bitter and became prone to angry fits of irrational behavior.

At age seventeen, Mindy found a haven in a mysterious man around town, but they never spoke, and Mindy held a secret crush on him for years. The eve of Mindy's nineteenth birthday, her mother was at a charity event and too busy to bother with her. So she went out with a friend and spotted the man. He had smiled at her and she was about to introduce herself, when her mother came home from the party and saw her. Elaine had leapt out of her car, marched over in her high heels, and told the man to never speak to Mindy again. Then, she had slapped Mindy across the face and ordered her to get in the car. Humiliated and bewildered, Mindy had ridden home in silence with her mother, packed her bags, and left. It was later that she found out that Elaine was jealous of her beauty and wanted no competition.

Sighing, Mindy put her head in her hands, trying to forget the dark memories that washed over her. Thankfully, she was jarred out of her morose reverie by the sound of her phone going off. Checking her text, she saw that it was from Belinda, giving her the directions to the Redwood Lounge. With a teary smile, Mindy texted a thank-you to Belinda, grateful that she was going out tonight, able to forget her mother. With another jaded sigh, Mindy pushed herself up off the bed, going to her suitcase to find something to wear. Since she didn't care about being too fancy, Mindy picked a black stretchy t-shirt and jean capris, putting on a pair of black flip-flops and tossing her hair back into a ponytail. Even though she wasn't extremely dressed up, Mindy always looked very nice when she went out. Checking the bedside clock, Mindy grabbed her purse and headed out of her room, taking the elevator down to the lobby. Looking out the glass doors,

Mindy saw that it was still a beautiful, sunny day, though the sun was heavily listing toward the western sky, beginning to turn red around the edges. Enjoying the breeze when she stepped out, Mindy walked to her car and climbed in, figuring that the Redwood Lounge shouldn't be too hard to find.

There was a moderate amount of traffic near the downtown, and Mindy was held up at a few lights before she finally made it to the pub. The Redwood Lounge was a long, low building with its own parking lot and a neon OPEN sign in the window. Mindy parked and reached for the glass door, surprised by how chilly it was inside the restaurant. Looking around, she saw that there was a restaurant section with black tables and dark wood walls with red lamps hung from the ceiling. At the far end of the room there was a bar counter with a list of draft beers posted on the wall behind it. Mindy decided that the place was retro in kind of a Goth way, but it seemed to be a decent place.

Mindy hovered near the hostess stand, scanning the darkened room for a sign of Belinda. Finally, she heard someone calling her name and saw Belinda waving at her from a table near the wall, a bottle of beer in her hand. Relieved to have come to the right place, Mindy cut across the room and seated herself across from her friend.

"Hey, hey," Belinda greeted her cheerfully, standing up to meet her. "I'm sorry you couldn't find me right away! I hope your drive here was okay." Belinda was dressed in a silky, flowy flowered top and leather motorcycle pants, with her black hair piled high on her head. Her green eyes were sparkling and her lips were stained cherry-red to match her fingernails and new red stiletto heels. Adding to the look was a pair of feather earrings that fell nearly to her shoulders. Smiling, Mindy was impressed by her new friend's eccentric, out-of-control-chic style.

Mindy waved a hand. "Don't worry about it," she reassured Belinda. "I found it just fine. Thanks for inviting me out."

"You needed a proper welcome to Vermont," Belinda explained, smiling at Mindy. "And I needed a new friend." She lifted a hand in the air and waved at a passing waiter. "Hey, waiter," she called, motioning him over.

The waiter, whose name was Trent, came over and smiled at Belinda, looking both her and Mindy over generously as he handed out menus, "What can I get for you ladies?"

"I'll have a bottle of Pacifica and a glass with ice to start, please," Mindy requested.

Trent turned to Belinda. "Any more drinks for you, Miss?"

Belinda shook her head. "Nah, I'll just have a plate of Spaghetti Nachos, please. Make enough for two."

Trent nodded and returned shortly with Mindy's beer, setting it down. He informed Belinda that the nachos would be a few minutes.

After Trent had left, Mindy gave Belinda a puzzled look. "Spaghetti Nachos?" she asked. "How does that work?"

Belinda put her hand on Mindy's arm. "Trust me, they are good," she said in a conspiratorial tone. "And hey, did you notice how he was checking you out?"

Mindy took a swig of beer and laughed. "Well, tell him I'm not interested," she said gaily.

Belinda studied Mindy across the table. Why, do you like someone else?" she asked with a smile.

Looking down at the table, Mindy shook her head. "Yeah," she admitted softly, smiling faintly as she pictured B.'s handsome face.

Belinda sensed the wistful tone in Mindy's voice and smiled at her. "Hey, it's never too late," she said wisely. "Who is this guy you've got your sights on? I thought you didn't date."

Mindy laughed. "I don't," she replied. "And this guy, I guess he's different. You probably know him, though."

Belinda shrugged and took a sip of her beer. "Dude, so what if I do? I won't tell him, I promise. I'm on your side, girl."

Mindy squinted at her. "You won't steal him either?" she asked mock-suspiciously.

"You have my word," Belinda assured her. "I wanna take Clay home tonight," she tossed her hair with an exaggerated flick and gestured to a tattooed busboy carrying a heavy tray of dishes. When he passed, Belinda smiled at him flirtatiously and he responded with a wink.

"Do you know him well?" Mindy wondered, now curious.

"Aw, yeah, I come in here very frequently," Belinda explained. "Besides, he's an old friend, graduated from the U," her face sobered and she wiped her face gently. "You know, ever since Brody dumped me, things are just different. I'll never have him back in the same way," she fell silent, a look of hurt crossing her pretty green eyes. Looking up, she met Mindy's eyes, a few lone tears running down her face. "It's just over."

Mindy reached over and squeezed Belinda's hand. "I understand," she said soberly, seeing the genuine sadness in Belinda's eyes. "Same sort of thing happened to me when I was nineteen. Only I never got to meet him. Life is rough."

"Indeed it is," Belinda took a long sip of her beer, shaking her head. Looking up, she smiled weakly. "Enough sadness tonight. I want to hear about this guy you like."

Mindy shrugged and blushed. "His name is B. Fairmont. He owns the Manor House coffee shop," she explained. "Do you ever go there?"

"I had a feeling it was him," Belinda replied with a knowing smile. "He's a sweet guy. You guys would be perfect together."

Mindy gave Belinda a strange look, wondering how she knew. As she opened her mouth to ask, the waiter brought a tray of Spaghetti Nachos and set them down in front of the two ladies with a plate for each of them. "Here ya go," he said cheerfully, and departed back into the kitchen.

Picking up a nacho with her fork and taking a delicate bite to try it, Mindy glanced across the table at Belinda. "How did you know?" she asked with a trace of suspicious astonishment. "Do you know him well?"

Belinda finished a nacho and wiped her mouth. "Yeah, I know him pretty well," she replied. "And I was there the day you slipped."

Mindy shook her head. "Why didn't you tell me?" she demanded, sounding harsher than she needed to. "I thought you looked familiar."

Belinda smiled and shrugged. "Never came up in conversation, I guess. Besides, I wasn't entirely sure, and I didn't want to freak you out."

Mindy laughed. "I'm sorry, I didn't mean to yell at you," she apologized. "But tell me about B."

Belinda waved her hand. "Don't worry, I deserved that," she chuckled. "But one thing I will tell you is that the day you slipped, I saw the chemistry between you two, felt it in the air," she smiled softly. "It was an extraordinary sight."

Surprised, Mindy wiped her mouth on her napkin. "You think so?" she asked. "I was just trying to recover from making an idiot of myself."

"Don't quote me on this, but I think he likes you," Belinda reassured her, giving her a secret smile. "If you want, we can head over tomorrow morning and grab a coffee or something from your beau."

Mindy blushed again and shrugged. "Sounds great," she agreed. The two of them talked for quite a long time over the plate of nachos and ordered ice cream and coffee for dessert. Belinda wouldn't go into too much detail about B., but she explained that he was nothing more than an old, close friend. After their beers had worn off, maybe around ten o'clock, they decided to head out.

"Thanks so much for dinner, Belinda," Mindy told her. "I had a great time."

"Same here," Belinda agreed as they left the restaurant. "I'm so happy to have met you, Mindy. I'm off this week, so just text me tomorrow and we can ride over to the Manor House, and maybe do some more shopping after. If you have other plans, just tell me."

Mindy shook her head. "Nope, sounds like an awesome idea," she told her friend. "I'll see you tomorrow."

Chapter Ten

The next morning was as sunny and beautiful as the others had been, and Mindy was amazed at how a city could be so constantly sparkling with sunshine. In New Jersey, she would be lucky to get five sunny days a year, or so she thought. As Mindy rinsed off in the shower, she was both excited and nervous to be going out with Belinda to see her beau. Mindy felt a tingle of anticipation flutter in her stomach as she pictured B.'s handsome face, kind, wise eyes, and feathered brown hair, along with his rock-solid body and brawny, tattooed arms. Realizing that she was dallying in her daydream, Mindy finished in the shower and dried herself off, wrapping her hair in a towel turban. Barefoot, she padded into her bedroom and thought about what to wear, deciding on a casual baby-doll style light blue printed camisole and comfortable black sport shorts that clung to her hips. Then, she put on her black flip-flops and twisted her hair back in a hairclip, fastening topaz drop earrings in her ears for an extra flair. Cleaning off her glasses, she slipped them out of the case and put them on, placing them so that they rested just below the bridge of her nose. Mindy had a habit of scrutinizing people over the frames of her glasses, which she fondly referred to as her "librarian habit."

Once she was dressed, Mindy brushed her teeth and took a long drink of water to rinse her mouth. Pulling her scratched flip phone from her purse, she texted Belinda and told her that she was ready to go. Since they would spend most of the day together, they decided to ride together. Within a few minutes, Belinda pulled up in front of the hotel in a sleek black sedan. Mindy rose from her chair in the lobby and went out the glass doors to meet her friend.

"Hey, you look great," Belinda exclaimed as Mindy slid into the passenger seat. Belinda had the radio on low and Mindy could hear the thumping of the beat of some song. Belinda herself was dressed in a stretchy gray t-shirt and black shorts, the outfit being surprisingly subdued for her. But true to Belinda style, she had her black hair piled high and her lips sealed with red to match her red earrings and red silk scarf.

"Thanks, Belinda, so do you," Mindy replied enthusiastically as she fastened her seat belt. "I'm so glad we could do this."

Belinda smiled as she turned the corner. "I am too," she answered. "I haven't seen B. for quite a while. He's such a cool guy."

"Indeed," Mindy breathed, a tender smile blooming across her face.

Belinda said nothing but gave Mindy a knowing look as they turned the corner and began to ascend the hill toward the Manor House. It was a lovely morning, the mountain air washing crisp and cool across their faces as the sun streamed down from above. There was a slight breeze in the air, and as they got higher up the hill, they could see some gentle whitecaps cresting on the deep-blue surface of Lake Champlain. In the distance, remote jade-green mountains rolled into infinity, and the city pulsed with life on this early morning. Mindy pondered all of this as Belinda pulled into the parking lot beside the quaint old house and cut the motor.

When they got inside, the place wasn't too busy, and Mindy immediately looked around the room for B. She knew he was there, because his presence had wound around her like a mystic wind the moment she and Belinda had opened the door. Looking by the window, Mindy felt her heart rate speed up as her gaze locked onto the man of her dreams. He was sitting at his usual window table, sipping on a cup of black coffee and concentrating on the book he was reading, his wise eyes pensively scanning the lines of text. His messy brown hair was naturally windblown by the oscillating fan in the corner, and the power of his gaze was shielded by his reading glasses.

When he looked up from his book and looked at Mindy directly, she felt her vision blur and she swayed unsteadily on her feet, frozen in awe of the sparks of wisdom and attraction sparkling beneath the calm surface of his gray eyes. With his usual serene half-smile, he lifted a hand and Mindy couldn't keep the grin from breaking out on her face.

As Mindy and Belinda joined the line to get some coffee, Mindy was aware of every sense in the coffee shop, the rich, smoky smell of Arabica beans and doughnuts in the air, the echoing chatter of customers and scraping of chairs against the hardwood floor, the sun streaming in through the windows. In addition to the usual heavenly coffee shop sights and sounds that she loved, Mindy could feel the subtle burning heat of B.'s gaze lingering on her as she made her way up in the line. She imagined how it would feel if it were his tough, work-worn hands tracing the curve of her hips as he gave his soft murmur of approval. Smiling, Mindy stepped up to the counter to order her coffee. She noticed that the same heavy-set girl was working there, looking more petulant than the day before. "May I help you?" she asked in a bored tone, wiping her hands on her apron and giving Mindy a slightly disdainful stare.

Mindy didn't let the girl's sourness dampen the tingling excitement she felt from being close to B. "Medium cinnamon latte with two shots and extra whipped cream, please," Mindy told her, sliding her card across the counter.

"Four-twenty," the girl replied, swiping the card and handing it back. With a more pleasant tone, she asked Belinda what she wanted. Mindy was puzzled as to why the girl seemed to have something against her personally, and why B. would employ such a grumpy staffer. As she pondered this, the girl finished whipping up her and Belinda's drinks and set them down on the counter without a word.

Without giving her a second thought, Mindy picked up her latte and inhaled the sweet, spicy scent, imagining how good it would taste. Beside her, Belinda held an amaretto latte and a donut that she offered to share with Mindy. Mindy could see B. smiling faintly as he read his book and sipped his coffee. Feeling suddenly bashful, she shyly followed Belinda in his direction, trying not to grin like an idiot. But any hope of a subtle entrance was quashed when Belinda sauntered across the room and called out to B.

"Hey, hey, hey!" Belinda crowed with fond boisterousness, approaching B's table and clapping him on the back.

B. grinned and rose from his seat. "Belinda," he answered in way of greeting, offering her a fist-bump. "It's been a while. How's the U?"

Mindy stood to the side and clutched her hot latte, feeling slightly out of place. It was clear to her that B. and Belinda knew each other quite well, and she couldn't help feeling like an outsider as the two of them briefly caught up, talking and laughing. She felt a niggling of jealousy at the fact that she hadn't been noticed yet.

Seeming to sense her restlessness, Belinda gestured to her. "My new best friend," she announced proudly to B. "Mindy's taste in shoes is fabulous."

For the first time, B. lifted his eyes and met Mindy's gaze directly, a shadow of a faint smile lingering on his face. "I'll bet she does," B. replied to Belinda with an amused twinkle in his eye. Turning to Mindy, he dipped his head in greeting. "Mornin', Araminta," he said softly, the sound of her name on his lips sending a rush of pleasure up Mindy's spine.

Mindy blushed. "Good morning," she replied cheerfully, a grin breaking out on her face. "The coffee is awesome. Your place is so beautiful."

A soft glow of pride shone in B.'s blue-gray eyes, as it always did when Mindy complimented him. "Thank you," he replied sincerely. She loved his modest, almost bashful way of accepting her praise. Shifting in his seat, B. moved his plate and gestured for Mindy and Belinda to sit down in the chairs across from him. "You can sit if you like," he offered.

Mindy gracefully seated herself across from him, but Belinda shook her head. "Nah, you guys go ahead," she replied, giving Mindy a conspiratorial wink. "I'm gonna sit outside and finish some paperwork." She tapped her watch. "Deans work all the time."

After Belinda had departed with a flick of her scarf and a cloud of lavender body spray, Mindy and B. were alone. At first, Mindy felt somewhat shy without the aid of Belinda's exuberant personality, but B. put her at ease almost immediately.

"I see that you've met Belinda," he pointed out with a chuckle. "She's quite flamboyant for a college dean."

"Yep, definitely," Mindy agreed, taking a sip of her latte and smiling as she wiped her mouth with a napkin. "We became friends the moment we met in the shoe store." Mindy told B. how Belinda had convinced her to live in the moment and buy the shoes she wanted.

"That sounds like something she'd do," B. agreed fondly. "She's a cool person."

They sat in silence for a while, sipping their coffee and looking out at the picturesque mountains, comfortable to just enjoy each other's presence. Clutching her coffee cup, Mindy looked down at the table and wondered what the past had been between B. and Belinda. Finally, when curiosity overtook her, Mindy looked up at B.

"Have you known Belinda for a long time?" she asked finally, trying to keep the question casual.

B. nodded and sipped his coffee again. "Yes," he answered. "She used to come in here all the time when she was in college."

"I see," Mindy replied, interested. "Did you ever… date her?" the question slipped from Mindy's lips before she could stop herself.

"Nah, she's always been more like family to me," B. explained. "We kissed at a party once, but that was it."

With this clarified, Mindy visibly relaxed and enjoyed the sunlight streaming in the window. She and B. made conversation, soon losing themselves in another fulfilling discussion. As always, Mindy found herself caught up in the whirlwind of his colorful mind, amazed at the clarity and depth in which he reflected upon a variety of topics.

Stimulated by the intellectual intensity of their conversation, Mindy studied him as he spoke, captivated by his soft-spoken manner. When they came to a lull in conversation, Mindy let her mind wander, drinking him in as he gazed out the window. His soft brown hair was messy and lightly feathered, dancing ever so slightly in the occasional draft from the fan. His long-lashed eyes flashed with an infinite expanse of sensations when he explained a mathematical concept, and the sun was shining in through the window at the right angle to illuminate the intricate dragon tattoos on his brawny arms. Seeing the faraway passion in his eyes and feeling the aura of his sexy strength, Mindy could barely breathe. She couldn't explain the feeling of just wanting to hold him, let her soul touch his. She barely knew the man, but within three days he had shattered her reserve and she was facedown at his feet. Never before had she… wanted, a man so much.

"You seem to be deep in thought," B. remarked, an amused twinkle lighting his eye as he finished his coffee. "May I ask what so holds your fascination?"

With an embarrassed grin, Mindy blushed, hard, and brushed a tendril of hair from her face. "Just our conversations, I guess," she answered vaguely, though she knew her burning face gave her away. "You gave me some deep material to work with."

B. only smiled in response, a flicker of unbridled desire flashing strong in his eyes before he subdued it and his visage returned to normal. Mindy blushed again, feeling a flood of warmth rush to her untended core and remain, causing her to shift in her seat to accommodate the pleasant sensation. Finally, overwhelmed by the hot energy radiating between them, Mindy broke the silence by asking him what he was reading. Not only did it serve as a tension-breaker, but she genuinely wanted to know.

"This book?" B. asked, holding up the paperback novel.

"Yes," Mindy clarified. "What's it about?" she had noticed that the title was *Primrose X,* and it was written by a lady named Aimee Haslett Blackburn. Once she saw it, she was intrigued by the unusual title and unfamiliar author.

B. set the book down and explained that it was a futuristic novel about a mutated species of primrose which could cure serious ailments. The side effect was that the patient would randomly fall in love with someone within twenty-four hours. At first, it seemed like a miracle, until it began breaking up marriages and causing social havoc. It became apparent that the match was always impractical.

"That's amazing," Mindy breathed. "Your taste in books is something else."

"It's pretty good so far," B. agreed. "This young scientist is working with the plant, trying to further research it. I've gotten to the part where his wife gets sick and he needs to decide whether to use the plant."

"Wow, that's deep," Mindy commented. "I'd like to read it sometime."

B. smiled. "Well, I'll let you borrow it when I finish," he offered, running a hand over his hair. He pushed his chair back. "I want another coffee," he decided, standing up. "Can I get you anything, Araminta?"

"Well, I'd love another cinnamon latte, but…" Mindy sighed guiltily.

B. winked. "Another latte it is, then," he replied gallantly. "I'll make it myself."

Mindy started to protest, but he silenced her and went up to the counter, going through the gate marked *employees only.* Mindy watched as he casually strolled across the room, admiring his straightforward, cheerful gait. She could see his strong muscles shifting beneath the thin cotton of his t-shirt, and figured that he must do some heavy outside work to be fit like that. He was the perfect balance, trim but not too skinny, buff but not too beefy. Looking at him, Mindy realized that he wasn't a very tall man, maybe only 5'9, but he could carry it well with his compact build. She saw him smile as he went behind the counter and started making their drinks, emerging a few moments later with two tall to-go cups balanced on a tray, along with some sort of dessert on a plate.

Returning, he set it down on the table with a flourish. "My treat," he announced. "Custom made by the owner."

Mindy laughed and took her cup as B. sat down. Taking a sip, she closed her eyes and exclaimed aloud how good it was. "Man, B., what do you do up there?" Mindy exclaimed. "This is the best latte I've ever had."

B. coloured and grinned. "I've got my wicked ways, Araminta," he replied quietly in a completely serious tone, leaning back in his chair with his signature half-smile.

"Oh, I'm sure you do," Mindy breathed, her voice coming out soft and fluty. She blushed lightly as she thought about all the ways that they could be wicked together. Deciding to flirt with him a little bit, she lowered her voice and leaned forward slightly, causing her necklace to slap against her chest. "I bet you're good at everything," she told him, looking him on with veiled desire and sincere adoration in her eyes.

This time, his gray eyes flashed like lightning as he studied her, his eyes searching her face and lingering briefly on her cleavage before he returned his gaze to hers. There was a nearly visible jolt of electricity crackling in the air between them. He sucked in a deep breath. "Well, I do have many interests," he answered finally, his voice coming out hoarse. Mindy could tell that she had severely affected him, thrown him off balance.

"What kind of coffee did you make?" she asked conversationally, unable to handle the full intensity of his desire.

He shrugged. "I like it black," he replied, taking a sip of his coffee. "Simple, straightforward."

"I used to only drink black, too," Mindy agreed. "But now I'm an espresso-based maniac. I wish I knew your secret ingredient."

B. chuckled and shook his head. "Sorry, that's classified information," he grinned. "But if you want, I can teach you how to make a mean latte of your own."

Mindy beamed. "I'm in," she confirmed. "But I don't think I'm ready to serve customers," she added, still smiling.

B. took a sip of his coffee and shrugged. "No problem. I thought we could come in after hours some night. Belinda can come too if she likes."

Mindy felt slightly disappointed, hoping it would just be the two of them, but she figured that it would be quite fun with Belinda too. "I'll ask her," Mindy offered. "We're going shopping this afternoon."

B. shook his head. "With all the money that Belinda spends, it's a good thing she works as much as she does."

Just then, Belinda walked back in the door and threw her empty cup away. "How's it goin' over here?" she asked, stopping at their table.

"Great," Mindy answered with a smile. "B. just invited us to an after-hours latte training session. You in?"

"Absolutely," Belinda agreed, sighing. "This coffee is to die for!"

B. smiled and looked over the frames of his glasses. "How about Thursday, then?" he offered. "Everyone's usually out by seven-thirty."

"That sounds fantastic," Mindy breathed, a soft light glowing in her gray eyes as she looked at B.

He grinned and sent her a wink as he got up from the table and started stacking their dishes onto the tray. "Lunch rush is coming up," he observed, aiming his gaze in the direction of the growing lines at the counter. "I think I gotta do some crowd control."

"I'm gonna get another drink," Belinda announced. "I need at least three macchiatos to get through the day."

Chapter Eleven

After Mindy and Belinda left the Manor House, they decided to continue the extravaganza that they had started the day before… shopping. It was Belinda's favorite activity and Mindy grew to appreciate the uniqueness of the Vermont stores. Besides, Mindy had nothing else to do, so it gave her a great opportunity to get a guided tour of the city with a well-versed local. Not only did they shop, but Belinda showed Mindy around the city as well, stopping to explain certain sights to her. With the radiant summer day enveloping them as they perused the stores and the busy city, Mindy felt like she was in paradise. The feeling was completed when she had seen B., who was like paradise in himself.

Mindy was strolling along the boardwalk beside Belinda, letting the sun beat down on her and enjoying the sensation of the lake breeze ruffling her hair. Belinda was saying something, but Mindy was lost so deeply in her thoughts that she didn't hear. She was thinking about seeing B. and how he made her feel. His gaze burned her up and she felt completed, perfect, but at the same time she felt like she wanted to give him more. She wondered how it was that she hadn't been in love in ten years, but it had only taken a few moments with the charismatic coffee shop owner before she was falling for him.

"Mindy?" Belinda's voice broke the silence, pulling her out of her engaging thoughts. "Are you listening to me?"

Mindy shook her head. "I'm sorry, Belinda, I wasn't paying attention," she told her friend. "I was just thinking."

"You really like him, don't you?" Belinda's question came out of nowhere, causing Mindy to jump.

Mindy was silent for several minutes, a wistful smile blooming on her face. "Yeah," she answered finally. "I do." Belinda smiled faintly and squeezed Mindy's hand, and Mindy spoke again. "Do you think I'm enough for him, Belinda?" her voice came out shaky, unsure, and her eyes were misty. "I mean, I'm just a tourist."

"Mindy," Belinda's voice was soft. "I've known B. for a very long time. I wouldn't tell you this if I didn't mean it, but he's different with you. I've never seen him like this with anyone else. I think he thinks you're special."

"Oh," Mindy said softly, not sure what else to say. "Thank you, Belinda."

Belinda grinned. "Don't thank me, I'm just the messenger," she replied. "But where do you want to go?"

A faint smile came to Mindy's lips. "The bookstore," she decided, thinking that she could get another puzzle piece of B.'s life story by looking up his favorite author.

"Cool," Belinda agreed. "I need some books for the rest of my vacation."

They agreed, and set off for the book shop, a quaint nook on the corner of the pedestrian street. As they walked through the door, they were met with a welcome blast of air-conditioning. "Ah," Mindy sighed. "That feels great."

"I know," Belinda agreed. "I was beginning to worry about sweat stains," she wrinkled her nose, adopting a mock-snotty air.

Mindy clapped Belinda on the shoulder. "Come on," she said with a laugh.

"Welcome back, ladies," the woman at the desk greeted them warmly. She addressed Mindy. "So, are you enjoying your vacation so far?"

Mindy nodded, having talked to her the day before. "I am," she replied. "It's so beautiful here." The women made small talk for a few moments before the desk clerk asked what she could help with. "I'm looking for a book," Mindy told her. "It is titled *Primrose X* by Aimee Haslett Blackburn. Do you have it?"

"Hmm," the woman replied, clicking into her computer. "Doesn't sound familiar, but I'll look it up. Do you know what year it was published?"

Mindy shook her head. "No, I don't," she replied. "My friend was reading it and he told me about it."

"Okay," the woman answered, typing something into the monitor. She searched for several minutes until she finally looked up with a regretful expression. "I'm sorry," she told Mindy. "We don't have it."

"Do you have any other books by that author?" Mindy wondered.

The woman shook her head again. "No, I'm sorry. Perhaps try the public library or look it up online."

Mindy thanked her, and then decided that she wanted to search the library database. She and Belinda left the bookstore and walked into a small café next door that had free internet access. "I'm really curious," Mindy said to Belinda once they were seated. "They didn't have it."

Belinda shrugged. "That happens, I guess," she pulled out her phone. "I'll try the Burlington Public Library website."

"Okay," Mindy agreed. "Cool. I'll get us some drinks while you look it up."

Belinda opened her browser and began searching while Mindy went up to the counter to order some drinks. This café, called the Lakeshore Café and Bakery, was nowhere near as nice as B.'s Manor House. Looking around, Mindy could see the vast difference in class. The Manor House was beautifully built, with original crown molding and all the charm of an old house while being modern and hip at the same time. The atmosphere at the Manor House was almost addicting, flooded with B.'s intense charisma. This café, however, was in an old storefront building, with far less charm and effort.

Still, everything in the city had a certain magic to it that just wasn't found in New Jersey, or anywhere else. Nothing in the city seemed rundown or depressed; everything was glowing with summer and vitality.

Up at the counter, Mindy ordered mineral water for her and Belinda, deciding she was sick of coffee. The line had been rather long and the café was crowded, so it took a considerable amount of time to get back to her table. Once she had paid for the mineral water, she brought the two chilled bottles back to the table and set one down in front of Belinda, who was deep in her search and didn't look up. Leaning back in her chair, Mindy yawned and ran a hand over her hair, then popped the cap of her mineral water and took a grateful sip. When she set the bottle back down on the table, Belinda finally looked up, startled.

"Oh, Mindy, you scared me!" she exclaimed. "I didn't even hear you come back."

"Sorry about that," Mindy replied. She gestured to the cold glass bottle. "I hope mineral water is okay."

Belinda nodded. "Great," she answered, twisting off the cap and letting out a refreshed sigh when she took a drink. "I love this stuff."

The two of them chatted for a minute before Mindy glanced at Belinda's phone. "What did you find out?" she wondered.

Belinda wiped her mouth on a napkin and folded her hands in front of her. "Well, it's the oddest thing. I searched the Public Library Database to start, and it wasn't there," she began.

Mindy furrowed her brow. "That's weird," she commented. "I don't know why it's so hard to find. Is it out of print?"

Belinda took another sip of her water. "That's the thing, Mindy, it gets even weirder. I looked up Aimee Haslett

Blackburn on the search engine, and nothing. No biography, no mention of her at all. It was literally a blank page."

"No way!" Mindy exclaimed, choking on her mineral water, causing Belinda to lean over and whack her on the back. Once Mindy stopped choking, she bit her lip and frowned. "I wonder how B. got the book, then."

Belinda shrugged. "I don't know," she answered. "He doesn't talk about himself very often."

"I know," Mindy replied softly, running her finger over the surface of the table. "It's like… he doesn't trust anyone."

"I don't blame him," Belinda replied. "Trustworthy people are hard to find."

The conversation continued in this vein for a few minutes before the two of them began to talk about other things. When they were finished with their mineral waters, Mindy and Belinda got up and decided to continue shopping, this time for clothes and shoes.

"Have you heard about the Sunset Beach Gala?" Belinda asked excitedly as she and Mindy were strolling along the street.

Mindy shook her head. "No, I haven't," she responded. "What's that?"

Belinda grinned. "My favorite part of summer. Every summer, in mid-August or September, the mayor of Burlington hosts a gala on the beach at sunset. There's a barbecue, a live band or DJ, a dancefloor, and an auction. We party 'til the sun goes down, and then the pink spotlights come on for the last dance," Belinda sounded out of breath with excitement. "It's magical."

Mindy smiled wistfully as she imagined it. "Sounds awesome," she grinned, giving her friend a sideways glance. "Will you go?"

"Duh!" Belinda exclaimed with a wide smile, smacking her forehead. "And you're gonna go too! We just need to get you an outfit. Dress is semi-formal."

"Where should we go?" Mindy wondered, deciding to trust Belinda with the task of finding a good shop.

Belinda thought for a moment and snapped her fingers. "Summer Nights," she answered, gesturing to a boutique farther down the strip. "They have formal, semi-formal, anything. It's probably my favorite shop."

Mindy smiled. "Let's go," she agreed, looping her arm through Belinda's.

The two of them set off down the street, enjoying the glow of the late-afternoon sunshine coming down on them. A gentle breeze rippled through the trees and Lake Champlain's sparkling dark waters were visible in the distance. "What a perfect day," Mindy commented.

Belinda took a sip of her mineral water, which she had taken with her from the café. "Summer in Burlington is paradise," she agreed. "I love it here."

The two of them made casual conversation as they walked along the cobblestone street, taking time to look in the windows of all the shops. Finally, they reached the boutique in question and went in, causing dainty bells to jingle when they opened the door.

Inside the store, Mindy looked around, amazed by the variety of clothes they had. Rows of colorful sundresses hung on one rack, color-block skirts and shorts on another, lacy tank tops, jean capris, tourist T-shirts, sunglasses, shoes, and jewelry. The store itself was nicely furnished, with glossy wood floors and interesting artifacts hung on the walls. "Holy crap," Mindy breathed. "I've never seen a store like this. Is it expensive?"

Belinda shrugged. "It can be," she replied. "But they do have some great clearance stuff. This is the perfect place to buy a Beach Gala outfit."

"I'd say," Mindy remarked as she fingered a silky skirt. Looking at the price tag, she frowned and flipped it over.

"Just be you," Belinda advised. "I'll give suggestions if you want," she lifted a fist in the air. "We're gonna blow out this beach gala!"

Then, Mindy and Belinda parted ways and began to wander around the store, occasionally consulting each other for suggestions. Belinda dug through the clearance rack and came rushing up to Mindy, excitedly brandishing a cherry-red fringed kimono with a gold dragon on the back. "Check this out!" she crowed. "It's on sale, too! Now I just need something to wear with it."

"That's awesome," Mindy commented, thinking about how it would perfectly compliment her friend's dark look. The two of them shopped around until Mindy found a dark gray skort and a matching gray camisole, both adorned with hints of red ribbon. She held the outfit up for Belinda's examination, and Belinda beamed.

"I love it!" she exclaimed. "This will go perfectly. Let me just pop in and try it on."

Mindy waited while Belinda went in the changing room and tried on her new outfit. Mindy knew it would look good, but when Belinda came out of the dressing room, she looked stunning. The red offset her dark hair, giving her almost an Asian look. The gray kept the look grounded, softened the contrast as opposed to black. "Also, I plan to wear an onyx necklace and earrings and put a red feather in my hair," Belinda added as she gave a model-spin for Mindy.

"Wow," Mindy agreed. "Definitely a keeper. You're gonna run the town."

Belinda grinned and went to change back into her regular clothes, appearing a moment later with her new clothes on their hangers. "Okay," she said when she rejoined Mindy. "Now that I'm taken care of, it's your turn."

Mindy smiled. "Sounds good," she answered. "I'm not much of an expert in dressing up."

"Never fear," Belinda spoke in a mock British accent and gave a grand, sweeping bow. "The Dressing-Up Expert is here to assist you." The two of them burst into laughter. "In all seriousness, though, I'll help you out," Belinda offered. "I know we can find something, you're beautiful."

"Thanks," Mindy smiled at her friend. "You are too."

With a smile, Belinda asked Mindy what colors or styles she liked to wear. "We need to find something uniquely you," Belinda thought aloud. "This is the biggest event of the summer."

"Well, I like plain colors and pastels," Mindy offered. "I don't really wear red, green, or yellow."

"Okay," Belinda agreed, focused intently on the rack. "I'll work with that. Just look for something you like and go try it on."

Mindy perused the racks for quite some time, managing to come up with a few options. She was never very talented in fashion, especially when it came to dresses. The few times a year that the bank would have an event, Mindy would throw on her only black cocktail dress and black pumps, never really having to think about it. But this was different. In this case, Mindy actually wanted to dress up, to make her statement at the Burlington Beach Gala. Looking down at the pile of dresses in her arms, Mindy decided that it was time to go try some of them on. "I've got a few," Mindy told Belinda, showing her the pile. "I'm gonna go change."

"Okay," Belinda agreed absentmindedly, still sorting dreamily through the clothing racks. "I'll be right here."

Mindy went to the back of the store and entered the wooden door marked FITTING ROOM. She closed the door behind her and hung her selections on the wall to be tried on. Stripping off her street clothes, Mindy took down the first dress and slipped it on. It was a tea-length, spaghetti-strap sparkling turquoise sundress, and Mindy thought it might work. But when she zipped it up and looked in the mirror, she shook her head and quickly took it back off. *This dress makes me look like a mermaid,* Mindy thought to herself. While looking like a mermaid wasn't necessarily a bad thing, it wasn't the image that Mindy wanted. After years of being a banker, she was used to more sophistication than that. Mindy tried on several more dresses, unable to find one that she truly liked. The sand-colored silk slip she had picked made her look washed out, the lilac boatneck looked weird, and navy blue just didn't quite cut it. Frustrated, Mindy changed back into her clothes and barged through the door, dumping the pile of rejects onto the return rack. Belinda looked up from where she was trying on a feathered beret. "How'd it go?" she asked Mindy with a serene smile.

Mindy lifted her empty hands. "I can't find anything, Belinda," she grumbled. "This is why I hate dress shopping."

"Whoa," Belinda held up her hands. "Have patience. There's gotta be a dress here for you. In fact, while you were changing, I picked out a few things that I thought you might like."

Mindy watched as Belinda flourished and held up two dresses. On the left was a silk slip similar to the sand coloured one, but it was in peach. It was a pretty dress, with a strapless bodice and a mid-thigh-length flowy skirt. On the other side, Belinda held up a black cotton V-neck dress that flowed to just above the knees. Around the neckline, sleeves, and hemline, there was a delicate trim of pale peach ribbon, same color as the other dress.

"Damn, Belinda, where did you find those?" Mindy wondered. "They look great."

"I'll let you in on a little secret," Belinda leaned forward. "I minored in textile design in college. I know a thing or two about style. Hope you enjoy."

Mindy gratefully accepted the dresses and went back to the changing room to try them on. Feeling more optimistic, she shut the door behind her and took off her t-shirt and shorts once more, deciding which dress to try on first. Since the peach silk dress was in front, Mindy tried it on first. As she zipped up the back and faced herself in the mirror, she nodded with approval. The style and cut were all nicely becoming, the silk skirt swished to just above her knees. Making a final adjustment to the strapless top, Mindy stepped out to let Belinda give her opinion.

"That looks really nice, Mindy," Belinda remarked. "Though I can't make a fair judgment until I've seen the other one."

Mindy nodded in agreement and went back into the booth to try on the other dress. She took off the peach silk one and hung it back up, trying on the other dress.

As soon as Mindy had on the other dress, she made her decision. While the peach silk one had been very pretty, this one was stunning. The soft black cotton showed off her tiny waist and slim figure, falling delicately to her knees. The material was comfortable; casual enough for a beach party, and the peach trim was beautiful. Mindy decided that she liked the traces of peach better than an entire dress of that color, preferring a sleek, sophisticated black. Smiling, Mindy stepped out of the dressing room and was met by a gasp of amazement from Belinda.

"That dress was made for you!" Belinda exclaimed. "It's absolutely perfect."

Mindy beamed and spun around for her friend. "I've come to that conclusion myself as well. You're a genius, Belinda!"

"Okay, Missy, go bag up that gown so we can finish your outfit!" Belinda jokingly shooed Mindy back to the dressing room. Always efficient, Mindy returned a few minutes later with the dresses in her hands, hanging up the peach one on the rack and taking the black one with her. When she came out, she found Belinda already checking out the accessories. "I'll hold that for you," Belinda offered, taking the dress from Mindy.

"Thanks," Mindy replied as she looked for the perfect complement to her outfit. They looked around for a few minutes, Mindy looking at jewelry and hair accessories while Belinda looked at shoes. "I've got it!" Mindy called, holding up a shell-shaped barrette that almost matched the trim on her dress.

"It's beautiful," Belinda agreed. "It adds a relaxed, beachy vibe to your black dress."

"I know, it's exactly what I'm looking for," Mindy replied. "I'm planning to go simple with the jewelry, dangling silver earrings and my silver cross necklace."

"You've got serious style," Belinda said admiringly. She slung her arm around Mindy's shoulders. "Come on. They have some great shoes here."

Mindy smiled shyly. "I'm wearing my silver sandals," she told her friend. "The ones we bought together."

"Awesome," Belinda replied. "You'll blow everyone away, including B."

Mindy blushed. "I hope so," she said softly. "I know he'll blow me away."

Belinda's eyes softened. "He won't be able to stop looking at you." Then, she returned to her usual cheerful manner. "Now let's go check this shit out and we can go out for lunch."

Chapter Twelve

The week went by quickly, and Mindy thoroughly enjoyed each relaxing day. Her days were like heaven: coffee in the morning, sightseeing, swimming, and blowing money with Belinda. Before she had come to Burlington, Mindy didn't know that life could be this enjoyable. She was used to working and not really having much fun, but as soon as she stepped down on the Vermont soil, everything changed. The city was like a fresh rush of energy that revived Mindy's dulled-out senses. And in the essence of the city's vitality was the mysterious, charismatic man that Mindy had found herself falling in love with.

Looking at the display on her scratched old cell phone, Mindy saw that it was Thursday. This was the day that B. had invited her and Belinda after-hours to make lattes. Mindy smiled at this thought, tucking a stray wisp of brown hair behind her ear. She had just gotten dressed, having showered after her morning workout. Today, her outfit was simple but classy: a blue ruffled scoop-neck t-shirt and a pair of white cargo shorts, only accessorizing with her simple sterling-silver cross necklace, which had been a gift from her father. Looking out the window, Mindy gazed out at the sunny courtyard, amazed at how a place could be so beautiful every day. Ever since she had been in Burlington, it had been yet to rain, each day as magnificent as the last. Putting her hair back in a loose ponytail, Mindy turned away from the window, checked her reflection in the mirror, and sat down on her couch to read the newspaper.

Just as Mindy sat down, her cell phone started ringing. With a frustrated sigh, Mindy got up and fished it out of her purse. Checking the screen, she saw that it was Belinda. "Hey, Belinda," she answered, brightening when she realized that it was her friend. "What's up?"

"Well, I have an awesome idea for today," Belinda announced excitedly. "I just thought of it this morning."

"Cool," Mindy replied. "Let's hear it!"

"You know how B. invited us out tonight?" Belinda began.

"Yeah?"

"Well, I thought that we could just hit the drive-thru at the Manor House today. That way, we'd give him a little glimpse, but he'd miss you until tonight. Believe me, guys like that sort of thing," Belinda explained conspiratorially.

"That's brilliant," Mindy answered enthusiastically. "You're a wise woman, Belinda."

Belinda laughed. "I do my best," she remarked. "Even college can't teach you the art of courtship; it's a battlefield that you have to navigate on your own."

"Again true," Mindy replied rather wistfully. "I wish it was easier, but I guess it's good to know the game. What time do you want to go?"

"I'm ready anytime," Belinda answered casually. "I'm still on vacation, so I don't really have plans."

"Perfect," Mindy agreed. "Just come on over."

"Okay, I'll be there in ten minutes," Belinda responded. "See ya soon."

After Mindy had hung up with Belinda, she grabbed her purse and headed down to the lobby to wait, idly flipping her keys in her hand as she rode the elevator. As the elevator touched down on the ground floor, the doors opened with a cheerful *bing* and Mindy stepped out, striding energetically across the lobby so that she could watch for Belinda.

In a few short minutes, Mindy saw Belinda's sleek black sedan slide up to the curb, clearly hearing the reverberation of the mega-bass stereo. Mindy slung her purse on her shoulder and rolled her eyes in the direction of the heavy-set male desk clerk who was blatantly checking out her butt. Briskly, Mindy strode through the automatic doors and shielded her eyes from the bright sun, lifting a hand to wave to Belinda. Belinda honked cheerfully and excitedly waved Mindy over to her car. Mindy grasped the polished silver door handle and slid into Belinda's car, impressed by the comfortable leather seats and clean, new-smelling interior.

"Hey, nice ride!" Mindy exclaimed as she shut the door behind her and fastened her seat belt.

"You like?" Belinda grinned. "It's new, this year. I got sick of cruising around in a piece of shit, so I surprised myself." She paused. "Besides," she added dryly. "My car should last more than a couple months, unlike my jackass ex-boyfriend."

"You really know how to deal with crap, Belinda," Mindy remarked quietly with a smile. "It's impressive."

Belinda secured her jet-black hair in a hairclip on top of her head before backing out and heading down the road. "Thanks, but it's probably just jaded bitterness," she answered, holding a bobby pin between her teeth as she drove with one hand.

"Maybe; Maybe not. Do you want to date again, ever?" Mindy asked cautiously.

"I'd just like to be married," Belinda said softly, keeping her gaze on the road. Sensing that her friend was upset, Mindy decided to let it go and changed the subject, commenting on the beautiful weather. Belinda quickly returned to her usual animated self, chatting away as they headed up the hill towards the Manor House.

"I just have all these… feelings, about seeing him," Mindy remarked with a nervous laugh. "I almost can't look at him, he's so brilliant."

Belinda smiled. "Must be love," she responded thoughtfully. "Just be you."

With that, Mindy looked in the mirror and adjusted her ponytail, admiring the artless, wind-tossed look to it. For a last-minute addition, she swiped her lips with chap-stick and put the mirror back up. "I'm ready," she told Belinda with a grin. "Let's go get 'em."

Belinda flicked on her turn signal and pulled into the Manor House driveway, lining up for the drive-thru. There was a large silver van ahead of them, so it was a minute's wait. Finally, when the other vehicle moved, Belinda cruised up to the window and rolled her window down. The window was at the moment vacant, and Mindy could see B. at the sink, putting something away. She felt a twinge of excitement at seeing him, and hoped that it would be him that would take their order.

Almost as if he felt Mindy's psychic plea, B. turned away from the sink and came up to the window, brushing a hand over his feathered brown hair. "'Morning, ladies," he grinned as Belinda leaned out to bump fists with him. Mindy smiled shyly, trying not to stare in mindless awe at him as Belinda ordered her drink. He certainly looked magnificent today, she thought to herself. The morning sun was shining in the window, illuminating his face as he held up his hand to shield his eyes. As always, his gray eyes were sparkling with kindness and live wit, and his tortoise-shell glasses made him appear older and wiser. He was dressed in a loose, soft-looking dark-blue T-shirt with VERMONT printed in white letters on the front. Through the soft sleeves, Mindy could see the outline of his muscular biceps, adorned with his mesmerizing tattoos. She was lost so deeply in her reverie that she didn't notice that he was waiting for her order, a faint smile hovering on his lips.

"Dang, I'm sorry, I got distracted," Mindy murmured with a short laugh. "I'll have a large cappuccino with extra whip, please."

"That'll be three-fifty," B. said, flashing a rare smile in Mindy's direction. He studied her for an extra beat, amusement and fascination twinkling in his eyes. "I'll be right back."

Mindy couldn't stop looking at him as he turned away and began whipping up their coffees, grinding the espresso beans and whipping the steamed milk with a strong, level hand. A moment later, he returned, passing the drinks through the window. Mindy and Belinda each paid for their coffees and B. took a moment to print out their receipts.

"So, are we still on for a late-night latte lesson tonight?" Belinda asked him, relieving Mindy of the question that had been burning in her mind.

B. grinned and hit print, pulling out the receipt. "Of course," he answered. "The place should be cleared out by seven-thirty."

"Perfect," Belinda agreed. "We'll be here."

"See you tonight," Mindy beamed, giving B. a cheerful wave.

B. waved back. "You two enjoy your day," he replied. Looking directly at Mindy, his friendly smile softened ever so briefly before he turned away and Belinda headed out of the driveway.

Once they were back on the road, Belinda turned to Mindy with a pensive expression. "He thinks you're special, Mindy," she said quietly.

"Really?" Mindy wondered hopefully. "Every time I try to be myself, I end up looking like a freak. I'm not used to this dating thing."

Belinda smiled faintly. "It's simple. You're in love with him," she pointed out, casually steering with one hand.

"Perhaps," Mindy replied softly, not really looking at Belinda, her gaze fixed on the amorphous, never-ending hills in the distance.

The two of them rode in silence for a while, enjoying the cool, fragrant lake breeze that was drifting in through the window. "Hey," Belinda suggested finally. "Want to go boating today?"

"That sounds like fun," Mindy replied, letting the breeze whip her light brown hair around her face. "I didn't know you had a boat."

Belinda shrugged. "It's just a small one," she answered. "But plenty of fun nonetheless. Want to head down to the marina?"

"Sure," Mindy agreed. "Except for the ferry, I've never been on a boat before."

Belinda looked shocked. "Are you serious?" she sputtered. "Dude! You're definitely missing out! Let's go!"

The two of them headed down to the docks, and Belinda parked her car. When they got out, Mindy was amazed by how perfect the day was. The lake was a deep, velvety blue with gentle waves washing to shore. The brilliant, bright sun streamed down in the nearly cloudless sky, reflecting off of the surface of the water and illuminating the mysterious sage-green coast in the distance. A few sailboats cruised in the water, propelled along by the gusty, sea-scented breeze. Several boats were moored along the docks, and Belinda led the way to a medium-sized, three-seat boat with a retractable canopy. The name emblazoned on the side was "Study Hard" and Mindy laughed at the ironically academic name.

"Welcome aboard the Study Hard," Belinda adopted a tour-guide tone; stepping into the boat and helping Mindy get in as well. "I'm Belinda and I'll be your captain today. Life jackets can be found in the back."

"Yes, ma'am!" Mindy saluted, putting on a life jacket and handing one to Belinda. "Ahoy!"

Once they were vested, Belinda leaned over to unhook the mooring and started the engines with a roar, jolting Mindy back in her seat as she pulled away from the dock.

"Yes!" Mindy yelled as a wave of droplets sprayed up, cooling her with a slight mist. "This is so much fun!"

"Told ya," Belinda responded from the helm.

"So, how'd you learn to drive a boat?" Mindy wondered. "You don't seem like the type."

"Appearances can be deceiving," Belinda replied with a smile. "My father was an ex-navy man, and when he moved to Burlington with my mother, he became a fisherman. I practically took my first steps on a boat. I went with him on all his adventures, and he had me able to command a ship by the time I was fifteen."

"Wow," Mindy breathed, amazed. "You're so diversely educated. That's so cool."

"I do love learning," Belinda replied, shading her eyes from the sun. "Let's put the canopy up." She pressed a button and the taupe canvas canopy blocked out some of the heat of the sun, while still affording a pleasant view.

They boated for quite some time, and Belinda pointed out various landmarks to Mindy, spouting out interesting facts. *She really does make a good teacher,* Mindy thought as she looked fondly at her friend. Mindy loved the splash of the waves against the hull, the heat of the sun searing through the canopy, and the hypnotic motion of the boat. Most of all, she loved the sight of beautiful Burlington on the shore, glowing with just as much radiance as it had on the day she arrived. Looking over, Mindy thought of B., trying to see if she could see the outline of the Manor House up on the hill. She wondered if he was thinking about her, if he was looking forward to their evening as much as she was. Her heart skipped a beat at the thought of seeing him again, and she wondered what it would be like to be on a boat with him, just the two of them in the middle of the lake, far away from civilization.

When they had had enough, Belinda checked her watch and steered the boat back to the shore, both of them excitedly remarking on how much fun it was.

By the time Mindy returned to her hotel room, it was nearly five-thirty. She was out of breath and flushed from her boating extravaganza with Belinda, and had thoroughly enjoyed herself on the ride. Looking in the mirror, she decided that she certainly needed to wash up and change her clothes before going over to the coffee shop. Not only was she soaked with waves of lake water, but she smelled like the sea and her hair was wildly mussed by the wind. Heading to the bathroom, she stripped off her clothes and left them in a pile in her laundry bag. She grabbed a white fluffy towel off of the rack and stepped into the shower to relax and clean up before her plans for the evening.

An hour later, at six-thirty, Mindy had finished her shower and taken a brief nap, and was just now getting ready. Propping herself up off of the couch, she yawned and padded over to her closet and suitcase, trying to figure out what to wear. *I need something that makes a difference,* she thought, wanting to dress her best for B. She shuffled through her small selection of clothes, quickly deciding on a soft cotton V-neck black shirt matched with lightweight khaki shorts and a pair of simple, classy black sandals. Reaching into her suitcase, Mindy pulled out one of her two sets of nice lingerie: a black lace bra and matching underwear. Smiling, she slipped these garments on and was amazed at how striking she looked. The black lacy cups held her meager curves in the most flattering way, and the delicate cut and translucent lace provided an air of demure mystery. *Perfect,*

Mindy thought. Next, she slipped on her shirt and shorts, one of her most flattering yet comfortable outfits. Once she was dressed, Mindy fastened sterling-silver drop earrings in her ears and hooked her cross necklace around her neck, with the pendant hanging down between her breasts. Then, she finger-combed her wavy brown hair and put it back in a simple ponytail, leaving wispy, curled strands to naturally frame her face. Finally, she put her glasses on and swiped some clear lip gloss over her lips. Once she was ready, she glided to the window and sat down on her bed, staring out at the beautiful evening, watching the sun turn golden in the cerulean sky. She had just picked up the newspaper when her phone went off. Fishing around in her purse, she saw that it was a text from Belinda. The message said that Belinda would be a bit late, and for Mindy to head over whenever she wanted. Mindy texted back and checked the clock, seeing that it was almost 7:00.

With a light sigh, Mindy rose off of the couch and made her way to the door, switching out the lights as she left. By the time she was climbing into her car, she was jittering with anxious excitement. She figured that she'd sit at a table until closing if there were still people there. She was secretly thrilled and kind of terrified that Belinda would be late, giving her time alone with B. *Breathe*, she told herself as she backed out of the hotel parking lot. *Just be yourself.*

With evening traffic rush in Burlington, it took maybe fifteen minutes before Mindy was ascending the hill toward the Manor House. The road wasn't as crowded as some of the town's main roads, and Mindy found it a pleasant, scenic drive with the lake breeze blowing in through her open window. As she came to the crest of the hill, the Manor House came into her line of sight. The beautiful old house was shrouded in just enough trees, and the golden sunlight was casting its shadow onto the western face of the building. Out front was a beautifully tended garden and canopied porch, with a majestic view over the valley. The sign in the window clearly indicated CLOSED, but Mindy knew it was open for her. The parking lot was barren and peaceful except for a souped-up, dusty burgundy pickup truck that she assumed to be B.'s. Smiling, Mindy turned the corner and maneuvered her rental sedan in the space next to the truck. Through the window, she could vaguely see a figure moving around inside. Checking her appearance one last time, Mindy shouldered her purse and stepped out of the car, gently closing the door behind her. Her sandals clicked softly on the pavement as she crossed the parking lot and ascended the stairs. Standing outside the door, she could hear soft strains of stirring music. Silently, she opened the door and stepped into the café, immediately met with the rich scent of coffee beans and glazed sugar. Looking up, Mindy caught sight of B. at the far end of the room, with his back to her, sweeping the floor.

Mindy didn't alert him to her presence yet, for it was a miracle to watch him work. The sun glinted in through the window, turning his hair golden-brown, and he bobbed his head to the lounge-rock song on the radio. His movements were measured and graceful; he moved across the floor like a sinuous flame. Mindy was riveted by his charisma, for he could appear captivating no matter what he did. She stood there for several seconds just taking him in, surrounded by the aromatic aura of the coffee shop.

Eventually, B. stopped sweeping and slowly turned around to face Mindy. His gray eyes sparkled and he lifted a hand. "Hello, Araminta," he said in his usual mellow, cheerful manner.

"Hey, B." Mindy replied, giving a nervous laugh. "I hope I'm not too early."

"Not at all," B. replied softly, his gray eyes glowing with veiled intensity. She saw his gaze flicker over her, lingering ever so briefly on the scoop of her shirt before he continued. "I was just cleaning up. Come on in."

Mindy smiled at him, her cheeks burning red as she felt the heat of his gaze sear a straight path up and down her body. "Belinda will be a bit late," she offered, her voice coming out husky and unpracticed. "I can help you clean up."

"If you want to," B. responded, smiling faintly as he carried the broom over to the corner. "You can start wiping off the tables while I clean up these dishes. There's only a few left."

Mindy complied, finding the checkered dishrag on one of the marble-topped tables. While she was wiping down the table, B. walked over to the bins of dirty dishes in the corner and stacked two in his arms, his tattooed biceps straining expertly against the load. "Holy hell," Mindy breathed softly to herself as she gazed at him, unconsciously dropping her dishrag onto the tabletop. She couldn't take her eyes off of him until he disappeared behind the kitchen door.

When he returned, Mindy looked up from the table and smiled at him coquettishly. "You're so efficient," she said softly, her eyes veiled with desire and admiration. "I'm very impressed."

B. smiled faintly. "Thank you," he replied modestly, though Mindy could see her desire mirrored in his eyes, hidden only by a fragile veneer of self-control.

Mindy started wiping the tables, listening to the faint sounds of the radio mixed with the hum of the electric fan and the banging of pots and pans in the kitchen. Through the opening in the kitchen door, she could barely see B. moving back and forth as he cleaned up the dishes.

This is so perfect, Mindy thought, letting out a sigh of contentment. She thought of her summer in Burlington and how everything seemed to be going right. Mindy turned to scrub the other side of the table, her back facing the kitchen as she gazed out over Lake Champlain. Her peaceful reverie was interrupted moments later by the sound of soft footsteps behind her. At first she continued to think, but then she became aware of a tingling energy gathering in the air. Turning around, she saw that B. was only a few feet from her with a spray bottle and rag in his hands, washing the windows.

"I didn't even see you there," Mindy told him with a laugh. "You're so quiet."

B. chuckled and spritzed ammonia solution onto the glass. "Habit, I guess," he responded good-naturedly, scrubbing down the window. "You seemed pretty deep in thought, though. I tried not to bother you."

Mindy shook her head and smiled. "It's okay, I was just thinking about the city," she explained softly, twisting the dishrag in her hands.

B. put the bottle down and turned to face her, his mysterious gray eyes deep with unexplainable waves of emotion. "And?" he whispered hoarsely.

Looking into his eyes, Mindy felt like she was drowning in the depths of him. "Burlington is beautiful," she murmured, sharing her deep thoughts with him. "I can feel it, it's like it holds this ancient magic…" she trailed off, looking up at him. "You probably think I'm crazy."

"Araminta." Before Mindy could breathe again, B. murmured her name, causing all of her senses to go haywire. He was so close that she could see the rise and fall of his chest, feel his powerful energy radiating off of him in waves. His scent was most fascinating; he smelled of smoky Arabica beans, glazed doughnuts, and Indian summer. Closing her eyes, Mindy inhaled him and felt a heady rush as she leaned in. Desperate, she waited for the moment when his lips would engulf her in flames…

"Sorry I'm so late!" Mindy's paradise was broken by the sound of Belinda's voice. Her eyes flew open and she stumbled back from B., who quickly feigned washing windows. Looking up, she saw Belinda standing in the doorway with her hand over her mouth. "God, I'm sorry," Belinda said. "I didn't realize…"

B. set down his cloth and waved to her. "No worries, Belinda, we're just cleanin' up." He sounded nonchalant, and Mindy couldn't help but to feel a little bit hurt. Hadn't he felt anything from their near-kiss?

"I had to do my laundry," Belinda explained breathlessly, dumping her purse onto a vacant chair. She looked pretty in a rumpled way, dressed in a long, floral high-low dress with a studded leather belt, her hair clipped up artlessly with a large bow. "The place was about to close."

Mindy smiled at her friend, not wanting to look at B. "We're glad you're here," she lied, pulling Belinda into a side-hug. What she was really thinking was, *Damn you, Belinda! He was just about to kiss me!*

B. finished wiping down the windows while Belinda chattered excitedly to Mindy for a minute. When everyone was settled, B. set down his cleaning equipment and invited the two girls behind the counter. "Alright, who's ready to be a barista?" he asked with a twinkle in his eye, tossing a black apron to each of the girls.

"Meeee!" Belinda squealed, tying up her jet-black hair.

"I am," Mindy echoed more quietly as she fastened the apron around her tiny waist.

"Okay," B. said softly, brushing a wisp of his feathery hair from his face. "Coffee is a very complex thing. First, you have to decide what kind you want. There are three categories of roast: light, medium, and dark, and several types and brands of each."

B. led them to a closet, with shelves and shelves of coffee. "If you want a lighter taste, you'd want a light roast, like Ethiopian or Guatemalan," he held up two cans and set them back down. "Medium roast, I'd stay with House, it's the best. You won't want Costa Rican, it's too sour. That's why I stopped carrying it."

"Oh my gosh!" Mindy commented. "I don't like Costa Rican either! They had it everywhere in New Jersey. You finally get it that that stuff is terrible."

"I couldn't agree more," B. replied with a soft smile just for Mindy. Then, he returned to a more explanatory tone. "And of course, there are dark roasts; Columbian is the most common." Again, he looked at Mindy and winked. "And as I remember, Araminta has a penchant for Columbian coffee."

Mindy blushed and laughed as she remembered the day they had first met, how she'd decorated his floor with that same Columbian coffee.

After B. finished explaining coffee roasts, he talked about espresso, the base of all lattes and cappuccinos. Mindy listened and studied him, in awe that such a strong, charismatic man would be interested in something as delicate and domestic as coffee. Still, it didn't diminish his masculinity but amplified it.

Mindy got lost in her own thoughts, swaying gently to the music playing overhead. As she became distracted, she fell behind on the conversation, leaving B. and Belinda chatting like they'd known each other forever.

Looking over, Mindy saw B. helping Belinda try to grind espresso beans. Belinda was laughing and pressing on the lever in vain, and B. was shaking his head and coaching her, smiling with amusement. She overheard something about Belinda helping in the shop in the winter, and Mindy frowned. *I'll be gone in the winter,* she whispered to herself. Not wanting to ruin the mood, she turned and silently excused herself to the ladies' room.

While she was in there, she thought about all of her insecurities, about being a tourist and wondering if she really fit in at all. She was dreading having to return to New Jersey, to her dull, oppressive life. As she stood near the sink and sloshed water back and forth over her hands, Mindy thought about these things. After a few minutes, she dried her hands off and reemerged from the bathroom. B. and Belinda noticed her absence and were happy to have her back. B. then guided her in making her very own latte, and she felt considerably better. But still, Mindy couldn't help but to be irritated with Belinda for barging in right when B. was about to kiss her. That raw, almost vulnerable passion in his voice when they talked about the city had disappeared, and his kindness was much more casually friendly. Apparently the interruption had rattled him, because Mindy could sense the misty barrier that had formed behind his eyes, hiding his secrets and concealing his emotions. He was still friendly and cheerful, but Mindy felt that he was troubled, shutting her out.

When they'd all finished making their lattes, they carried them to a three-top table near the window and sat down. They were there a few minutes when Belinda suddenly got up and checked her watch. "Holy crap," she remarked. "It's seven-forty. I had to be at my cousin's rehearsal dinner at seven thirty!"

B. and Mindy waved and bade her goodbye as a very unorganized Belinda barreled out the door and ran for her car. "I'm off like a dirty shirt!" Belinda hollered as she leapt into her sedan and roared out of the parking lot, honking in farewell. B. and Mindy sat in silence for several minutes in the wake of Belinda's boisterous departure. Mindy sipped her latte and B. gazed out the window, turned away.

Outside, the sun was beginning to set over Lake Champlain, turning the clouds pink as the fading rays cast their shadow over the water. The trees were darkening into silhouettes, and the traffic on the hill was gradually becoming an ambiguous outline. Mindy tasted her latte, savoring the sweet flavor, but her eyes were glued to B.'s elusive form. He sat turned away from her, gazing out the window into the sunset. The last of the light dulled his features into a shadowy blur, but the handsome outline of his face was still visible. Shifting in his chair, B. stretched his muscles, giving Mindy another view of his lean, hard strength. Mindy watched him quietly as he thought, seeming to be miles away in his own thoughts. Mindy sighed and ran her fingers through her light-brown bangs, just taking time to look at him. She didn't sense tension in B.'s silence, just peaceful thoughtfulness.

The silence was intensely reflective, and eventually Mindy felt the need to reach out to B., to make her presence known to him in his reverie. "Beautiful sunset tonight, isn't it?" she managed in a raspy voice, the sound of her voice cutting into the silence of the air.

"Indeed, it is," B. murmured, his gaze still fixed far away. "I love the transition from day to night; it's the rhythm of life."

Mindy couldn't agree more. Even B's voice sounded like a sunset. He himself reminded her of the rhythm of life. The way he spoke, the rise and fall of his chest, the heat that radiated off of him, this was life. Mindy swallowed hard, overcome with the need to press her body against his. "It's beautiful," she repeated shakily, tears pooling in her eyes. "We never had sunsets like this in New Jersey. It's a miracle."

This time, B. did turn around. He said nothing but gazed at Mindy with his intense gray eyes, as if he were deciding what to say. Finally, he broke the silence. "Would you like another latte?" he asked quietly.

Mindy nodded. "I'd love one," she answered, and she got up to follow him to the counter, watching the fluid movement of his muscular form.

"Would you like to make it?" he asked her with a faint smile.

Mindy shook her head. "Nah, I'll leave it to the pro," she replied, smiling at him. "No one can make lattes like you."

Still smiling faintly, B. moved behind the counter and started expertly whipping up the sweet beverage. "Let me guess, pumpkin and whip?" he wanted to know.

"Go ahead and give me extra whip," Mindy requested. "I've a bit of a sweet tooth."

B. pumped the syrup into the coffee, swirled whipped cream on the top, and handed it to Mindy. "I suppose I do, too," he answered, his eyes twinkling.

B. made himself a latte too and joined her on the other side of the counter. The two of them stood quietly, watching the last of the sunset and listening to the soft strains of music that was playing in the back. The radio seemed to switch to deep, stirring songs, further charging the atmosphere between them.

Mindy took a sip of her latte, amazed by how it could be so perfect every time. "Ah," she breathed, closing her eyes. "So good, B."

When she looked up, B.'s eyes had darkened to a hot gray haze, and he was breathing heavily. Mindy sucked in a deep breath and let it out again as he took her cup from her and set it on the counter next to his, their fingers brushing with an electric jolt. Then, he took her wrists with a light, strong touch and looped her arms around his neck. "Dance with me, Araminta," he whispered. "This is my favorite song."

Mindy gave a soft gasp as B.'s strong hands rested on her slim hips, searing holes through the fabric of her clothes. She was amazed how a man could be so literally hot, just burning with heat. She closed her eyes and let him lead her around the room, listening to the soft sound of the radio and the ragged swish of his breathing. Along with all that heat, were wisdom, strength, and a maturity that exceeded finite time. Gently, Mindy reached up and placed her hand over B.'s heart, letting his steady heartbeat guide her steps. "When I look at you, I see the sunset," she whispered in his ear, trailing her fingers down the side of his face. "I see life itself. That's you."

Mindy looked up and saw a storm of emotions swirling violently in his gray eyes, like waves cresting in the turbulent seas. This torrent was shielded only by his feathered brown hair and burgundy glasses. He seemed to be struggling for control, as the music came to a heartrending crescendo. Mindy's heart was pounding in anticipation and she was shaking with sensation that was zinging through the air. B. tightened his hold on her hips. In his eyes, she saw flashes of lightning over the waves. Tenderly, she reached up to touch his face again, his gaze searing a path straight to her core.

Suddenly, the spark exploded into an inferno as B. crushed his lips to Mindy's, pulling her tight against his rock-hard frame. Mindy clung to his shoulders with all her might as a cascade of light exploded behind her closed eyes. His lips were hot and soft, and she could feel her whole body being enveloped in flames. Along with the sensation of his lips on hers, she could feel every inch of him glued against her, sighing as she let her hands run over his biceps, relishing in his strength. Below, she could feel his steely heat pressing between her thighs, a sensation so far missed that she nearly cried with joy. Feverishly, she rocked against him, needing to get closer. He groaned into the kiss and tightened his hold even more, so that his erection was grinding against her and his strong hands were roaming over her behind. Finally, when they could breathe no more, the two of them broke apart and gasped for air. Mindy's hair was a mess, her heart was pounding, and she could feel her pulse hammering in her core.

B.'s hold loosened some, and he ran his hands up her sides, looking at her intensely for a moment before he lowered his lips to hers again. This time, Mindy trailed her hands up and down his back and chest, finding that he was even stronger than she had realized. She sucked in a breath as he too reached up her shirt and unhooked her bra, the touch of his hot, work-worn hands making her head spin. She felt as if she were in the center of an inferno, feeling nothing but the flames dancing around her. The radio played an explosively sensual melody, kept in time with B.'s hard, steely frame rocking against her. He held her breasts in his work-worn hands, groaning softly as he gently squeezed and twisted her nipples. The blinding addiction was all Mindy could seek, feverishly giving herself up to his hands, her breath coming in whispery gasps. In the heat of their passion, B. peeled his shirt over his head and tossed it on the counter, giving Mindy a full view of his spectacular physique. The shirt hit the counter with a soft *thump* and Mindy staggered slightly, feeling dizzy when she saw him smiling at her, shirtless. He was beautiful, hot and in perfect shape, with tattoos running up his sides as well as on his arms. All of his tattoos were blue, Mindy's favorite. He had quite a few tattoos but not too many. "God, B." she murmured, lightly trailing her hands over his chest. "You're blowing me away." He let her admire him, watching her with smoky eyes before he finally crushed his lips to hers once again. While they kissed, she lavished her attention on his brawny arms and spread her legs wider for him, loving the feel of his strong grip on her.

When they broke apart, Mindy sagged against the counter, out of breath from the barrage of sparks exploding through her body. Every inch of her was tingling and she could almost feel the burn marks from where B.'s hands had blazed their trail. Looking up at B., she saw him standing with his eyes closed, his chest heaving up and down, heat radiating off of him for a good four feet. He seemed to be struggling for control.

"Dance with me some more," Mindy whispered, propping herself up off the counter and gently taking his hands. He hesitated briefly before spinning her around for the final chorus. For several moments they just danced, their bodies pressed together, B.'s hands holding Mindy firm against him. "You're so beautiful," Mindy murmured, tracing the shape of his tattoo with the tip of her finger. "I love this house, B.," Mindy continued softly, looking up at the vaulted ceiling and crown molding. "How did you do it?"

Suddenly, Mindy felt B. stiffen beneath her and he stopped dancing. Looking up into his eyes, she saw that his gaze had gone stormy and cold. "What?" he breathed, his voice coming out as a raspy whisper. He looked sheet-white and all of his muscles were clenched, ready to bolt at any minute. "What are you talking about?"

Bewildered, Mindy stepped back, wondering how she could have upset him in such a short amount of time. "You built this house," she tried to explain, her voice coming out shaky. "I was trying to say it's beautiful," her words were making no sense. "I'm sorry if I upset you, I didn't know."

B. was looking down at the floor. "Araminta," he said softly. "I never said that I built this house."

"But you did," Mindy answered quietly, searching his face for an answer. "You told me."

"I need to go," was all that B. said as he started packing up his things.

"I…" Mindy tried, her eyes starting to fill with tears. "I'm sorry!" She grabbed his arm. "Please don't go!"

B. pulled his shirt over his head and grabbed his wallet. He was shaking his head and his face looked stricken. "No, I'm sorry, Araminta," he murmured coldly as they left the shop, his paces long and agitated. "You don't know who I am."

With that, Mindy helplessly watched B. lock up the shop, stride over to his truck, and roar away in a spray of dust and gravel. Feeling cold and lost, Mindy shivered and made her way over to her own car, looking up at the darkened old house for a minute before slowly and silently pulling out of the deserted parking lot.

Chapter Thirteen

Mindy was sleeping soundly, buried beneath many layers of blankets, with a pillow over her head. Her dreams were ambiguous, only a cloud of gray mist with garbled nonsense and fleeting faded pictures. A chill from the heart of winter itself bit into Mindy's circle of warmth and she huddled farther beneath the blankets, shivering and trying to warm up. Still submerged in her dreamland, Mindy lay motionless, searching for warmth. A steady pattering noise came from somewhere distant as wakefulness threatened to drag Mindy out of her sleep. Feeling like she was surging up through a current of dark water, Mindy's head reeled as she was pulled abruptly into reality by a persistent beeping noise. Confused and dizzy, Mindy's eyes flew open and she shot up in bed, whacking her hand down on the large black clock by her bed, silencing the noise. After shaking her head for a few moments to get her bearings, Mindy pushed a hand through her wavy, light-brown hair and passively looked around the hotel room, remembering where she was. The first thing that she noticed was it was actually cold, colder than she'd ever experienced in early September. *God, it must be thirty degrees in here,* she thought, laying back down under the thick comforter and trying in vain to warm her skinny arms. Looking out the window, she actually jumped with a start when she saw the rain streaking down on the pane of glass, the view obscured by the heavy storm. Mindy pinched herself and blinked to make sure she was actually awake. The entire time she'd been on vacation, it hadn't rained. But now that it did, it was like it made up for all those other days. The wind howled mournfully through the trees, whipping handfuls of leaves around in a damp whirlwind. The rain was coming down so hard that it sounded like a million blacksmiths were hammering their anvils atop the hotel's roof. Looking at the clock, Mindy saw that it was almost nine-thirty, but the sky was still almost dark, as if the day hadn't dawned yet.

Still feeling somewhat sleepy, Mindy pushed the covers back and stepped out of bed onto the floor, padding across the room into the bathroom. She flicked on the light and stared at herself in the mirror, uncomprehending. Her hair was matted and hanging down over her face and her eyes were rimmed red, her face dry and puffy as if she'd been crying. Her cheeks were sunken and her eyes were crusted with sleep residue. *I look like I've been in a train crash,* Mindy thought, trying to comb through her tangled mess of hair. *Did I hit my head or something?*

Mindy was distracted from her thoughts by a crisp *ding* from the other room. Still unorganized, Mindy headed into her room and located her phone, the source of the noise. Flipping it open, she checked the display and she had one new message from Belinda. Opening it, she read: HOW'D IT GO LAST NIGHT??? ☺

Last night? Mindy squinted to remember what happened. She had taken a powerful sleeping pill before bed and it must have delayed her memory. But as she stood there, in her nightgown, hair still falling down in her face, she remembered. Everything came back to her, the boat ride with Belinda, the latte lesson, and…

Mindy's breath hitched in her throat. No. it couldn't be. The waves of sensation when B. put his hands on her, how his eyes had sparkled in the dim light, how he looked like a golden god with his shirt off… Mindy had felt like she was in heaven, dancing in his arms, until it was all taken away. One word, one wrong move and he had turned from an inferno of summer bliss to the coldest winter one could imagine. Mindy shivered. The stiff, terrified look in his eyes was one of the saddest things she'd ever seen. What was it that he was hiding so frantically? she wondered. Why had her comment about the house set him off like that?

Under the hot water of the shower, Mindy lingered, and these questions raced through her mind. She never knew that it could be like this between a man and a woman. All feelings of love and romance, passion and devastation, had been locked tightly away since Mindy was seventeen. She was a woman of business, with a business mind. In Araminta Cullen's world, emotions didn't get in the way. That was until she met B., she thought. He had brought to life the flame inside her that had lain dormant for nearly ten years.

What am I going to do? Mindy thought as she shampooed her hair. She figured that she'd head over to the Manor House and try to set it straight with B., tell him that she didn't mean to upset him. When she got out of the shower and was drying off, Mindy decided that she'd better straighten it out with him before things got any worse. She put on her navy-blue and white striped shirt, and a simple pair of white shorts. Her hair was still wet so she twisted it back into a hairclip and secured her glasses on the bridge of her nose. With her necklace, socks, and sneakers, she was ready. With a pensive frown, Mindy slung her purse over her shoulder and stared out the window. The rain was still coming down in buckets, and Mindy didn't have an umbrella. Riffling around in her suitcase, she managed to come up with a light gray hooded windbreaker. She slipped the coat on and tightened the hood, figuring that this was the best she would get as far as rain protection.

Checking her appearance one more time, Mindy slipped out of her hotel room into the dimly lit hallway. There weren't many people around and all she heard was the muffled sound of her own footsteps on the carpeted hall. Turning right at the end, she boarded the elevator and rode down to the ground floor, feeling tired and weary without her usual morning coffee. At the lobby, she stopped in the breakfast room and poured herself a Styrofoam cup of black coffee before heading out to her car. The rain had abated slightly as she emerged from the double doors, but it was still a drizzle cold enough to chill her to the bone.

Shivering, Mindy climbed into her rental car, set the coffee in the drink holder, and turned on the heat. The thermostat in the car indicated that it was 46 degrees outside. It was really cold. As she drove along the rain-soaked streets toward the Manor House, she wondered what she would say to B. How could she apologize when she didn't even know what she did? Turning at the corner, she began to ascend the steep incline up the hill. Looking out the window, everything looked damp and gray, with leaves flapping wildly in the pouring rain, Lake Champlain rough and stormy. Even though the weather was terrible, Mindy felt a sense of power in the wind and rain. There was a driving force, energy to the storm. Mindy managed to reach the top of the hill through the heavy mist, and she pulled into the parking lot.

For a moment she only sat looking up at the old house. The usually mysterious, charismatic building simply looked desolate and empty in the cold rain. The lights were on inside but the usual warmth of the place was missing. With a heavy sigh, Mindy got out and made a mad dash for the door, hoping not to get soaked through.

Mindy stepped inside, pushing her hood back. The familiar smell of Arabica beans and powdered sugar met her nose, and she relaxed momentarily. But even right away, she knew it wasn't the same. The pulse of energy that surrounded the place was weaker, less concentrated. Mindy craned her neck and looked around, trying to see if she could see B. anywhere. But there were a few people standing in the way, so Mindy strained to hear his soft, low voice or his raspy laugh. She thought she heard him, but she couldn't be sure in the jumble of voices that filled the café.

At the head of the line, Mindy was both disappointed and relieved to see that B. was not behind the counter. She was relieved that she didn't have to think of what to say, but what she felt was mostly disappointment. She had hoped she could come in and that everything would be okay. Even to see his face would have made her feel better.

"May I help you?" the voice jarred Mindy from her thoughts and she glanced up to find the barista staring at her quizzically.

"Ah, yes," Mindy replied finally, her voice coming out hoarse. "I'll have a medium cinnamon latte, please."

The guy typed it into the computer. "Is that all?" he asked. This guy, a scruffy, college-age blond, was nowhere near as handsome as B. He looked young and indifferent, and his eyes didn't sparkle with the four seasons the way B.'s did. This made Mindy realize how different B. really was, and how she was terrified to lose him.

"Is B. in today?" Mindy inquired softly, even though in her heart she knew the answer.

She must have looked crestfallen, because the guy gave her a tight, sympathetic grimace. "Sorry, he hasn't been in all day," he replied, sliding Mindy's finished latte across the counter. "That'll be $3.25."

Numbly, Mindy paid for her drink and turned soundlessly away from the counter, feeling cold and lonely. The café was relatively empty, so Mindy gravitated toward the table that she and B. had sat at the night before, a small two-top near the window. She just sat down and began to sip her latte, tuning out the clusters of conversation around her.

She stared out the window at the rough, swirling waves on Lake Champlain, and her mind drifted to the night before. B.'s presence was so powerful, full of vitality and charisma. He had swept her off her feet, taken her to a new level when she was in his arms. Never had she wanted to be with someone as much as she wanted to be with him. Mindy grimaced as she thought of how their evening had ended, with him taking off in a frantic rush, leaving her all alone. The look she had seen in his eyes when she mentioned the house, he had looked terrified. That made Mindy wonder what he could be hiding. She suspected that a whole web of mystery unfolded behind his stormy gray eyes, yet she knew nothing of him except how magnetic he was, able to be hotter than the sun or as cold as a polar wind. As she continued to look out the window, the choppy waves reminded her of what she'd seen from B. the night before. In fact, the frustrated, turbulent current was the same as she'd felt when B. tore out of the shop. It fascinated Mindy how earthy B. was. He seemed to hold the energies of nature inside him. Glancing up, she noted the strong, sturdy beams of the house, standing firm against the tempest. It was all too easy for Mindy to picture B. as he built it, shirtless in the midday sun, driving nails into the ancient wood and creating the house's frame. The thought bothered her, she couldn't figure out why she felt so weird about the whole subject. It had startled her the way he had flared up, making her wonder what was going on. There was no way that B. had actually built the house unless he had built it in modern time, which seemed impossible. The building materials were outdated, and the style was reminiscent of the Victorian era. Why would he come up with such an unbelievable tale? But why did she want to believe it?

Shaking her head, Mindy stood up, unable to think about it anymore. Every time her mind touched on the subject, she found herself more deeply confused. Finally, she decided to finish her coffee and leave, maybe go run some errands.

***

For the rest of the day, the rain held little hope of letting up. It was coming down in straight, steady streams, a controlled cascade of moroseness. Mindy went through the motions of her necessary errands: she did her laundry, picked up some groceries, and took a trip to the bank to check her travel accounts. But as she did these things, she couldn't shake the chill of loneliness that permeated her to the bone. She had a feverish hope of running into B. around town, but as she expected, she was searching the rain-soaked city in vain. Around 5:30 PM, Mindy headed back to the hotel and worked off some of her frustrations in the fitness room. She ran hard, her feet pounding the rubber belt of the treadmill, trying to fill her loneliness with the screeching guitar riffs of her favorite band. After a strenuous workout, she headed back to her room to get cleaned up. By the time she was finished with her shower, she was exhausted.

It was around 7:00 PM when Mindy was sitting in her living room, staring out the window at the rain, which had slowed to a somber drizzle, the sky beginning to get dark around the edges. Struggling to keep her eyes open, she shivered and wrapped a blanket around her legs. The temperature had dropped even more and she had gotten chilled from the cold all day long. She thought about dinner, but wasn't hungry yet, so she settled on a cup of tea. Slowly, she sipped her tea and closed her eyes, listening to the soft strains of music coming from the radio on the other side of the room. The least she could do after a tiring, trying day was take a nap. Mindy had just started to drift into a pleasant semi-sleepy state when she was startled by the ringing of her cell phone. Her eyes flew open and she rooted around in her purse to locate the phone. A shiver of hope ran through her as she thought that it might be B. She didn't know why he would call, but her heart beat faster as she lifted it to her ear.

"B.?" she breathed before she could think. "Is that you?"

"Hello," a rough male voice grated through the speakers, much different than B.'s soft, insightful speech. "I'd like to talk to Araminta Cullen."

"That's me," Mindy murmured as her heart sank. "Who are you?"

"This is Troy Haverman from the bank. You remember me, right?" he asked teasingly.

Figures, it would be Troy Haverman, Mindy thought bitterly. The last person on earth she wanted to hear from. She had met the man once in the airport and never wanted to see him again. "What do you want?" she asked tersely.

"Now, Mindy, no need to get fierce," Troy's tone was mocking. "It seems that there's a little, um, situation at the bank. Some shuffling of management and whatnot," he paused for a dramatic breath.

"Give me the short version," Mindy huffed, not wanting to waste any more time with this idiot.

"Okay, then, Your Majesty," Troy countered, matching her huffy tone. "Mr. Dean retired. The new manager wants you back immediately, preferably tomorrow morning."

"What?" Mindy shouted. "Why?"

"Like I said, change of management," Troy sounded smug. "We'll pay your ticket if you get a flight for tomorrow."

"Wait a minute," Mindy snapped. "If the *Manager* wants me back so badly, why are *you* calling me after office hours? Isn't that a bit unprofessional?"
Mindy blew out a frustrated breath and looked up at the ceiling, waiting for him to continue.

"Well, um, it was kind of a last minute decision," Troy tried to sound authoritative. Then, he paused. "So, how's your vacation?" he asked lasciviously. "Sun tanning on the beach in a bikini, I bet you look fantastic," he drawled. "Wish I could see it."

"If you're through," Mindy said coldly. "I'll be calling the manager first thing in the morning. Goodbye."

Troy laughed. "Okay, so we agree. I'll be picking up your pretty little ass at the Newark Airport, 7AM."

Mindy slammed the phone down and sat back in her chair, scowling. What a perfect way to demolish her evening. *Obnoxious prick,* she fumed. She wanted to tell him to take his fancy desk chair and shove it as far up his ass as it would go, but she needed this job. One thing she knew, however, was that she wasn't leaving Vermont until she got confirmation from the manager that that's what she needed to do. She'd call and see if she could negotiate. And as a banker, she was naturally good at hard figures and logical arguments.

Once Mindy's initial irritation faded, it was slowly filled by a deep, empty sadness. She sat there until the sky fully darkened, numbly sipping her tepid tea. It was bad enough that things had been difficult with B. last night, but now she was going to have to leave Vermont. That thought itself struck a blade so deep within her that she thought her soul might split. In the few weeks she had spent in this magical place, she had been transformed from a gray shadow of a person to a woman of color and light. Long-lost, never-discovered parts of her had been drawn from hiding, made reality by B., who was an earthy, living miracle. And at this rate, she would be wrenched from a perfect relationship before it could even start. *One thing is for sure,* Mindy thought stubbornly, if not a bit wistfully. *I'm not going anywhere until I kiss him one more time.* The radio was still playing softly, and Mindy rose to go to the other window, feeling compelled to look out into the night. The city was shrouded in a gentle, misty haze, and the raging storm of earlier had slowed to a melancholy light rain, which was almost as bad, if not worse, for Mindy's mood. If the earlier gale was a torrent of frustration, this was like the heartbreaking embrace of star-crossed lovers. Mindy stood there for several long moments, watching the cars navigate up and down the rain-soaked streets. The traffic lights changed from green, to yellow, to red, and back to green again, while neon signs illuminated the businesses along the strip. This slow-changing rhythm was like the breath of the city, rising and falling. Mindy was transfixed by the peaceful rhythm until her eyelids became heavy and she fell asleep on her bed.

Chapter Fourteen

The next morning simply yielded a gray, hollow dawn, no great rainstorms or tempests. The wind was buffeting about slightly when Mindy awoke, and there was a heavy mist in the air, but the weather wasn't as violent as the day before. But as Mindy looked out the window, she thought that the silent, heavy gray day was almost more depressing than the fierce storm of the day before. If yesterday's storm was passion and frustration, this was listlessness. With a light groan, Mindy pushed the blankets aside and stepped out onto the chilly floor. *I'm gonna need a sweater and pants today,* Mindy thought, shivering. She washed up in the shower, unable to shake the chill from her body even under several minutes of hot water. When the water turned tepid, she shut the shower off and got dressed in a long-sleeve burgundy shirt and black stretch pants. Not wanting to bother with her hair, she twisted it back in her usual hairclip, still damp. Looking out into the blustery morning, Mindy pulled a throw blanket tighter around her shoulders and sat on the couch to decide what to do with herself. She felt cold and empty, and even the warm blanket and cup of hot tea she was brewing didn't help. *I miss him,* she thought, watching the wind rip handfuls of leaves off of the trees and send them skittering across the barren landscape. Mindy's body ached as she remembered all the places he had touched her, and she let out a light sigh of discontent that those places were now left cold. She sleepily closed her eyes and was about to take a nap when her phone buzzed with a text from Belinda. Opening it up, she read: WANT TO MEET FOR BREAKFAST?

That would be perfect, Mindy thought, and her grim mood lifted slightly as she texted her acceptance to Belinda. With a frown at the clock, she decided that she had to call the blasted bank before she could do anything. Most likely an irate team of people was waiting for her at the Newark Airport. Sure enough, she checked her phone and saw that she had missed twelve calls. *Shit,* Mindy cursed, dialing the bank number and lifting the phone to her ear. "Hey, it's Mindy Cullen," she said shortly when the phone had been answered. "I want to speak to the manager."

There was a pause and click as the line was transferred. "Catherine Carrera speaking," a woman's faintly accented, stern voice came through the line.

"I heard that I'm needed back at the bank, and had to be there this morning. But before I left I wanted to confirm with you."

"That is correct that you need to come back," the manager replied. "But I didn't say anything about this morning. I know your vacation was two months but we expect you back by Monday. Troy Haverman, your replacement, is totally overworked, and all of the departments are backed up."

Mindy cursed Troy under her breath, covering the mouthpiece. "I see," she said briskly.

"Monday," the manager repeated. "Mr. Dean had good things to say about you, Araminta. I hope you won't disappoint me."

Mindy grimaced. "I'll try," she murmured, feeling swamped with despair.

After she had hung up, Mindy sank back into the couch cushions. Now her entire trip was screwed up. The first time she had ever been happy in life, made friends, and fallen in love, now it was all over. Mindy resented being dragged back to her hellhole of a town like a recalcitrant child. *Fuck the bank,* Mindy thought. *I hate them all. Especially stupid fucking Troy Haverman.* Mindy imagined giving Troy a sound whack in the balls with her loaded briefcase the next time he made some lewd comment to her. *That ought to wipe the cocky smirk off of his face,* she thought with a bitter chuckle.

Mindy fumed for a few more minutes when her phone buzzed again. It was Belinda, asking Mindy if she still wanted to go out. With a heavy sigh, Mindy told her friend to just come over to the hotel and they could have breakfast in the dining room. Mindy was still slouched down on the couch in a depressed stupor, silent tears beginning to slip down her cheeks when she heard a persistent knock on the door. Mindy got up to answer it and Belinda came in trailing a cloud of floral perfume.

"My Lord, Araminta, what happened to you?" Belinda exclaimed, setting her purse carelessly down on the floor. Belinda was dressed in one of her usual eccentric outfits, a jade-green floral top and black and white striped pants. Normally, the combination would look ridiculous, but Belinda's dark hair and infectious smile made it a bold fashion statement.

Mindy shrugged listlessly. "Things just suck, that's all," she replied weakly, wiping her eyes on her shirt.

Before she knew it, she was being swept into Belinda's arms. "It's okay," her friend reassured her. "Now, dry your eyes and come with me. I know a great restaurant, and you can tell me what's wrong. That's not a request," Belinda's voice sounded stern but she was smiling.

Approximately fifteen minutes later, Mindy and Belinda were seated at a quaint seaside restaurant, with a booth near the window. The place was called Henrietta's, and it was a refurbished cottage that served hearty, home-cooked meals and lots of Vermont specialties such as maple recipes and fresh fish from Lake Champlain. The day was still overcast, but the lake was pretty nonetheless.

No sooner had they been seated as Belinda leaned on the table, her hands folded in front of her. She had a pensive look on her face as she took a drag of her coffee. "Start at the beginning," she urged Mindy gently. "Maybe I can help."

Mindy sighed and shook her head. Well, everything fell apart about the same time," she said flatly. "Bottom line is, B. and I had a disagreement, and then things went downhill. I love him so much… and I have to see him again."

Belinda put a hand on Mindy's arm. "Mindy, take a breath. Men often overreact. What happened?"

Mindy didn't even want to talk about it, but she didn't have any more to lose. "Well, after you left on Thursday, B. and I, we talked and danced, everything was great until I screwed up."

Belinda smiled. "I feel terrible that I interrupted your kiss when I came in. I had no idea. But he danced with you? That's so romantic. I'm glad I left you two alone."

"None of that matters now," Mindy replied. "I said something to him and he flipped out." Mindy didn't want to tell Belinda what she said, because she thought that it was personal to B., since it was such a strange tale. "I overstepped the line and made an assumption; I thought I heard him say something that he later denied." Mindy gestured weakly with her hand and closed her eyes. "I hate all of these dating rules."

Belinda blew out a breath and furrowed her brow. "Misunderstandings have some of the greatest power to ruin a relationship." She looked crestfallen. "It's tragic but true.

Besides, B. is known for being kind of defensive if you ask him too many questions. Just give him time, he'll come around."

"That's the other thing," Mindy murmured, running her finger along the burlap-style placemat. Her gaze was hooded, dejected. "I have to be back at work on Monday. I don't have time."

Belinda looked shocked. "What?" she wondered. "Why?"

Mindy shook her head. "New management. Some woman with a big agenda, I guess. Not to mention, a pompous asshole for a coworker." She relayed to Belinda what had gone down with Troy.

"Yeah, he definitely deserves a good whack in the balls," Belinda agreed, taking a bite of her waffle. She cocked her head and looked at Mindy. "You're still coming to the beach gala with me tomorrow night, right?" she wondered.

Mindy sighed. "What's the point?" she murmured.

"Come on!" Belinda urged. "It will be fun. We already bought tickets. And if the weather is crappy, we'll have it inside. It won't hurt."

"All right," Mindy relented, looking down at her untouched breakfast. "My pancakes got cold."

"Well, I'll just order you some more," Belinda replied gaily. "You're gonna need to eat or it'll be a long day."

Once it was settled that they'd be attending the gala, Mindy felt slightly better, but the chill still hadn't lifted from her shoulders. She listened as Belinda chattered blithely about the gala and the city history involved in it. Belinda had a degree in art history, so she was telling Mindy about all the styles of buildings in Burlington.

"Belinda," Mindy began. "Do you know when the Manor House was built? I just wondered."

Since they were on the topic, Mindy figured she'd find out what she could, without telling Belinda the precise reason she was asking. Belinda thought for a moment. "Well, you've come to the right person," Belinda replied. "I conduct an architecture tour for the university every June. The Manor House was built around 1894."

Though Mindy already had a fair idea, she visibly drew back from the news. "Oh, that's cool," she answered. "I love old buildings. Tell me about some other ones." Mindy kept Belinda talking but she didn't hear a word she said. She couldn't think with the questions relentlessly swirling around in her head. Why would B. tell her he had built the house? Why was it so believable? And then, why had he gotten so defensive? Either answer left Mindy at a crossroads, making her more confused and intrigued at the same time. If he had lied about building the house, why? It was clearly an archaic style and no one would believe it. And if he *had* built the house... well, that had to be impossible.

Chapter Fifteen

"Fucking unbelievable." Troy Haverman cursed, slapping his hand impatiently down on his desk. Beside him, the printer was sputtering out page after page of forms that needed to be filled out, documents that were well on their way to missing their deadlines. It was Saturday morning, around ten AM, and Troy was sitting in his office at the bank, working. This was all Mindy Cullen's fault, he thought. If she hadn't gone gallivanting off on her damn vacation, his department wouldn't be so backed up. Now, because of her, he was sitting under a mountain of papers this weekend rather than at his cousin's wedding in Florida, macking on babes on Palm Beach.

I was supposed to be getting some serious ass this weekend, Troy thought bitterly as he signed a document with an angry flourish. *Now all I've got is a serious pain in the ass!*

The prestige of taking over Mindy's department had quickly worn off, and the thought of working on Saturday while Mindy was on vacation fueled his temper. As he looked down and saw Mindy's chicken-scratch notes she had left, he felt himself getting riled up all over again. He'd never met anyone like Araminta Cullen before. She was cold and frustrating, and he'd hate her guts if only she weren't so damned beautiful. It enraged and aroused Troy how Mindy played Ice Queen, freezing him with every word she said. All the men around the office knew Mindy's reputation. She was a workaholic and brutally rebuffed any man who showed an interest in her. *If I got my hands on that pretty little broad...* Troy thought, letting his mind wander as he waited for the rest of the documents to print. He didn't know which he'd find more satisfying, throttling her for messing up his weekend or screwing her senseless. Come to think of it, Troy thought, he'd very much like to do both. He wanted to bend her iron will, get past her inflexibility. She was like a firmly locked door, and he amused himself briefly by imagining what lay behind that door. He chuckled as he thought of the venomous upbraiding Mindy would give him if she knew of his lascivious thoughts. He thought about calling her again just to have some fun while he waited for his papers to finish printing. Instead, he texted Catherine Carrera, the manager, and asked if she could get Mindy home any faster than Monday. His phone vibrated with an answer and he reached for it, accidentally tipping over his coffee cup. With a shouted curse, he jumped up and began to dab at the mess. Once the fiasco was over, Troy checked his phone and saw Ms. Carrera's aggravating news, that Monday was the next business day, so no.

Sometime later in the evening, a very frustrated Troy stuck his keys into the brass lock and shoved his way into his large house on the outskirts of town. The place was lavishly furnished, dark, quiet, and clean. Not too long after Troy set his briefcase down, he smelled gardenias and heard the clack of stiletto heels echoing across the parquet floor.

"Hard day, Mister Haverman?" Standing before him in her black ruffled maid's uniform, with her honey-brown hair pulled into a ponytail, was his sexy Ukrainian housekeeper,

Natalia. She had just moved from Ukraine and didn't speak very good English, so Troy was able to take some liberties as far as how she dressed and when she worked.

"Tell me about it," Troy grumbled, insolently handing off his coat to the housekeeper. "Get me a bottle of wine, Natalia, and bring it up to my study. Also, get your pretty hands ready because I want a shoulder massage."

"Yes, sir," Natalia's English was muffled and heavily accented. "I be there soon."

Later, even as he was sipping wine in his leather recliner and having his shoulders massaged by Natalia, Troy's mood was still foul. He tried to concentrate on Natalia, but behind his closed eyes, all he saw were the stacks of paper in his office… and Araminta Cullen's disdainful expression and pert body. He growled, feeling like a caged cat. One thing he knew for sure: Miss Precision (as his friend Sam called Mindy), hadn't seen the last of him.

Chapter Sixteen

The next morning in Burlington, Mindy awoke leisurely, stretched out comfortably in her plush bed. As her eyes flickered open, she took in the autumn sunshine streaming in through the hazy curtains. After the past few days of relentless, wintry storms, she was glad to see the sun back out. When she pushed the covers back, she noted that the air didn't even feel as cold. Perhaps it would be a decent day after all. Going to the window, Mindy pushed the curtains back and the full splendor of the day spilled into her room. The sky was clear and blue, with vagabond white clouds drifting around the edges, never blocking the sun. The sun itself was brilliant, streaming down to illuminate the trees and buildings of the city. The trees were beginning to lose their leaves, the first plumes of red blooming among the golden-green canopies. The few fallen leaves were swept up by a playful wind that sent them skittering back and forth across the busy streets. The energy of the city was calm and steady, and Mindy felt a pang of sadness when she realized that she wouldn't be there to witness the beautiful fall foliage, the slow transformation from a vibrant summer to a deep and meditative winter. *I love this place,* Mindy thought as she opened the window, letting the morning mountain breeze wash over her. Still, her moment was tinged with sadness.

Though the scenery was beautiful, she was realizing that in a few hours, she'd be back in the colorless hellhole that she had called her residence for the past twenty-seven years. Now that she had had a taste of the fresh summer air and felt the miracle of true love, she was aching to have to give it up. But if she wanted her paycheck, she'd have to make that sacrifice. *Speaking of love,* Mindy thought, and a vision of B.'s handsome face came into her mind. Oh, how she missed him, even though it had only been a few days. She loved the depth of the seasons in his eyes, the flecks of sunshine he seemed to carry around with him everywhere he went. He was one with the earth, and even the blue dragon winding sinuously up his arm was a manifestation of his quietly masculine, earthy strength. With a dreamy, mournful little sigh, Mindy leaned her head on her hand and continued to look out the window, just thinking about her situation. Her reverie was brief, shortly interrupted by the sound of her phone. *This better not be who I think it is,* she mumbled, not in the mood to deal with Troy Haverman. But when she checked the text message, it was from Belinda, bubbling with enthusiasm about the beach gala. Mindy smiled at her friend's contagious zeal and prepared to type her response when there was a peppy knock on her door. With a little laugh, Mindy crossed the room, still in her pajamas, and opened the door. Sure enough, there was Belinda, dressed to the nines in a long-sleeved gray shirt and a pair of ankle-length floral pantaloons. Her inky hair was long and loose, clipped up with a fresh rose in it. With her outfit, she looked like a cross between a hippie and a gypsy, but true to Belinda fashion, she was always able to pull it off.

"Beach gala. Tonight. Are you ready?" Belinda's eyes were sparkling and she was practically breathless with excitement.

Mindy looked down at the floor. "I hope so," she murmured. "But I have to leave tomorrow. I'll miss this city so much, Belinda."

Belinda's expression sobered. "The city will miss you too, Mindy. And so will I. promise me you'll come visit."

"Of course," Mindy said softly, allowing herself to be pulled into Belinda's arms. She laid her head down on her friend's shoulder and was silent for several moments, tears stinging at the corners of her eyes.

Finally, Belinda pulled away and regarded Mindy with a serious expression. "Why waste the last day worrying about going back?" she asked quietly. Then a smile spread on Belinda's face. "Not another word. We're going to make the best of it. Now get dressed and let me take you to the bagel house. You haven't been here until you've had one of Bagel Joe's handmade miracles."

Mindy perked up a bit and took her friend's advice. Looking out into the brilliant morning, she decided that this was going to be the time of her life, even for one day. *I will fully live each moment and cherish it forever,* she resolved, as she went in her bedroom to get dressed for the day.

True to her word, Belinda showed Mindy a good time, taking her down to the quaint lakeside bagel shop. Bagel Joe turned out to be a jolly Burlington native with white hair and a contagious smile. The place was nothing but a glorified shack, but inside it was adorably furnished like a summer cottage kitchen with a nautical theme. The interior was open and airy with white fans hanging from the wooden rafters, blue color scheme, and an unlimited view of Lake Champlain through cozy bay windows. Mindy ordered a pumpkin-chip bagel with whipped cream, which ended up being the best thing she had ever tasted. Belinda swore by pumpernickel with peach jelly, which sounded unusual but ended up being delicious as well. After they had finished their breakfast and said goodbye to Bagel Joe, Mindy wanted to wander the city a bit and see anything she hadn't seen. She and Belinda drove around the city, and under the brilliant sunshine, Mindy began to forget that it was her last day.

***

It was about 5:30 when Mindy was back in her hotel room, getting ready for the beach gala. The party started at 7, so she wanted to make sure she had enough time. *If I'm gonna do this, I might as well do it right,* she thought, secretly hoping that she might see B. at the party. Mindy had rinsed off in the shower and scrubbed with her favorite vanilla body soap. She proceeded to blow dry and curl her hair before putting her dress on. When she finished, she was amazed that she was able to make herself look so beautiful. The soft black cotton flattered her slender figure and fell gracefully to her knees. The pale peach-pink trim around the edges softened the look and provided a complement to her strappy silver sandals. Looking in the mirror, her hair fell in soft waves around her face, pinned elegantly to the side by her seashell barrette. Her blue-gray eyes were wide and misty, and her lips shone with a subtle, peachy gloss. She fastened her silver cross necklace gently around her neck and matched it with silver dangling earrings.

By the time Mindy was done getting ready, it was almost time to go. Looking out the window, Mindy saw that the sun was low in the Western sky, and it would soon be making its graceful descent into a ball of orange-pink flame.

Feeling both excited and apprehensive, Mindy made her way toward her car and followed Belinda's directions to Sunset Point Beach, where the party would be held. She texted Belinda and told her that she was on her way, and Belinda said she was already there. Squinting into the evening sun, Mindy drove slowly through the city, watching the golden orb glinting off of the buildings. She drove down to the beach area, and even from about a mile back, she could see the cars parking and elegantly dressed people getting out to go to the party. The women were dressed in semi-formal dresses of many colors, their hair fixed beautifully, clinging delicately to the arm of their handsome dates. Mindy parked on the street and sat in the car for a few minutes before she decided to get out. A well-dressed, laughing couple strolled by, making Mindy's heart ache. With a tentative look in the mirror, Mindy applied another coat of lip gloss and alighted slowly from her car. Under the gentle sunset sky, Mindy billowed toward the gates of the beach, her heels clicking softly on the pavement.

As she rose up the steps to the beach, the magnificent party came into view. The Blue Mountain Club, the place where the party was hosted, was alive with lights and color. Out back, there were steps that led down to the dancefloor right on the beach, with pink spotlights, a DJ, and the sound of the waves crashing in the background. Soft music was playing and several people were already out on the floor, swaying back and forth to the music. Other people dined in the restaurant, the rich aroma of food permeating the air.

As Mindy looked around, she felt uncertain, not recognizing anyone she knew. Everyone seemed to already be engaged in a conversation, already having fun. Not sure exactly what to do, Mindy ordered a glass of wine from the bar and moved out onto the terrace to watch the waves and colorful dancers below. She stood there sipping her drink, the lake breeze gently blowing her hair around her face and causing her dress to flutter gracefully around her body. She took time to enjoy the moment, feeling the life and magic of the city humming all around her. The music was stirring and Mindy felt herself start to sway in time with it, wishing she had someone to dance with. On the floor below, Mindy spotted Belinda in her flash of red, dancing exuberantly with a handsome man. Belinda looked up and beckoned Mindy down, but Mindy shook her head and smiled, preferring to stay and observe.

Eventually, Belinda took a break from dancing and bounded up the stairs, pulling Mindy into a flamboyant embrace. She looked lovely, Mindy thought, in her red kimono with her dark hair loose and dark eyes glowing with excitement. She grabbed a plate of nachos and stood on the balcony with her for a moment, persuading her to get something to eat and get into the party. Mindy went into the blue-lit bar with her friend and got a brownie to go with her glass of wine. She and Belinda caught up for a few minutes, and Belinda asked again if Mindy wanted to dance. Mindy shook her head, saying that she wouldn't crash Belinda's groove. "Besides, I like the fresh air," Mindy explained. "I'll be down after I finish my wine."

"All right, see you in a bit," Belinda said excitedly. "Just come down and you can dance with me!"

Mindy laughed and watched her friend swirl down the stairs. She wanted to stay and observe a little bit longer, enjoying the lake breeze. For several minutes, Mindy was watching the colorful dancers and listening to the music twine with the sound of crashing waves. She closed her eyes, letting the sensual sounds rock her. She had just about finished her wine and was about to put her glass away when she felt an unexpected shift in the current, like a pulse of electricity crackling along a live wire. This barrage of sensation flickered steadily before returning to normal.

"Araminta," she heard her name, felt the vibrations of his voice resonate through her entire body. Breathless with anticipation, she turned around to see B. standing in the shadows beside her, studying her with a hint of a smile resting on his lips. Mindy's mouth dropped open slightly as her gaze roved over him. He was dressed in a simple dress shirt and slacks, his shirt rumpled and open slightly at the collar. His short, feathery brown hair was wind-tossed, and he was holding a drink in his hand. Even though it was a formal event, B.'s formal attire took nothing away from his wild, earthy strength. His sleeves were rolled up at the elbows, revealing the ornate tattoos winding around his sinewy arms. The wind was ruffling softly in his hair, making him appear as a natural force himself. And most of all, Mindy felt the strong force-field of energy pulsing around him, radiating off of him like a heat wave.

"It's a beautiful party," Mindy's voice came out shaky. She was desperate to say anything, to diffuse some of the energy crackling between them before it overwhelmed her. "The weather, the view is majestic."

"Indeed it is," B. agreed, his misty gaze searing a path of flame up and down Mindy's body. "You look very striking tonight, Araminta." His voice was a husky promise, his eyes flashing with veiled desire.

Mindy suddenly felt as if all the air had dried up, though they were out on the beach. "So do you," she breathed, reaching out to touch B.'s arm. "I'm glad you didn't cover your tattoos."

B.'s eyes darkened with stormy passion, just as the music switched to an achingly sensual song. "Care to dance?" he asked, extending his hand.

Mindy put her hand in his and felt like she was gliding on air as he led her down the steps to the dance floor. She wrapped her arms around his neck and he placed his hands steadily on her hips, causing her heart to beat erratically as he began to move with her in time with the music. He was an awesome dancer, steady as the earth itself, gently but capably revolving with her in time with the music. His touch was soft and light, but electric, and with his steady hand he maintained that he was in control.

Mindy was in heaven as he spun her around under the stars, his hot hands sending continuous jolts of pleasure up her spine. Like a moth to a flame, she restlessly sought his warmth, letting herself be fascinated with the rhythmic rise and fall of his chest, the solid strength in which he held her.

As time went on, their embrace grew feverish, as Mindy trailed a wayward alabaster hand over the outline of B.'s tattoo. "You're so beautiful," she murmured with reverence. "I can't explain."

B.'s breath quickened and he tightened his grip on Mindy's hips. "Araminta," he murmured raggedly, struggling for control. Mindy could feel the pounding of his heart and the searing heat of him in a split second before he crushed his lips to hers. At the collision, the caged spark broke free into a raging inferno, obliterating all of Mindy's senses with pure flame. This was not a gentle kiss, but a fierce passion like a winter storm. Mindy moaned softly as B. ravaged her mouth with his tongue, cupping her behind to hold her against him. She gasped again as she felt his erection between her legs, and her core was inundated with a flood of wet heat. Mindy kissed him just as ardently, pressing herself desperately against his steely heat. He groaned softly, tilting his head back as he pulled her closer, molding her shape to his. Desperately, his hands slid up her sides to hold her breasts and Mindy moaned, wanting nothing but his hands on her bare skin. He kissed her deeply, squeezing her breast hard though her dress as she ground against his leg with restless abandon. They danced fiercely, all sharp turns and heavy, flashing bursts of passion. Mindy was electrified by the energy radiating off of B., that burning supernova just for her. She didn't know if she could take his heat, but goddamn it, she wanted to.

"Oh, B.," she gasped as he leaned her back. Her legs were locked around his and her hands gripping his brawny arms. She loved the feel of him, all hard and hot, every inch of him all over every inch of her. She was lost to the world, aware only of his burning hands and the rhythm that they created. He took her higher and higher, and she ached for the final point, when she shattered in his arms.

Like a wake-up call, the songs changed from slow and sensual to upbeat and peppy. "I need another drink," B. told her brusquely, disentangling from her arms and heading off at a fast pace. Mindy shook her head dizzily and looked around, realizing that she and B. had nearly made love in a public place. Luckily, no one seemed to be watching. As Mindy stood still amidst the mass of gyrating bodies, she felt cold. Scanning the crowd, she hoped that B. would come back soon so that they could dance and talk some more. She separated from the crowd and started to ascend the stairs, going after B. But as she looked around the bar, she realized that B. wasn't with them. She was standing on the balcony when a figure caught her attention. Though it was dark, Mindy could barely make out B., shifting his way through the crowd with his powerful shoulders, heading toward the gate.

Mindy's hand flew to her mouth and her eyes stung with tears when she realized what was happening. B. was leaving her, again!

"Oh, no," she moaned aloud, tearing away from the balcony and breaking into a run despite her heels. She barreled down the stairs and slogged through the sand, trying desperately to catch up with B., who was walking at a clipped pace and had almost reached the gate.

"B.!" she screamed, hoping he would hear her, but the sounds of the party were too loud and her call was lost. Just when Mindy thought she may have a chance of catching up with him, B. broke into a brisk jog at the bottom of the steps and rounded the corner.

Chapter Seventeen

Everything was pounding. The drumming of his feet on the pavement matched the sound of blood rushing in his head as B. broke into a light run. He had torn away from the beach party, knowing he needed to get home before things got too hot.

Damn it, he cursed softly as he jogged along. The night had been just about perfect. The gala was beautiful, right at sunset, the food and music were sublime. Perhaps the best and worst part of the evening was Araminta, all dressed up in that sinuous black dress, her hair curling softly around her face. She was so artlessly beautiful, and she bloomed like a flower every time he came around. B. groaned as he thought about how they had danced; she wound herself around him and gazed into his eyes with her unwavering icy blue ones, revealing the hidden promise of her desire. He saw it in her eyes, she ached for him, wanted him physically as bad as he wanted her. And more than that, there was a giddy tenderness in her eyes that could be called love. But that expression he'd seen in her eyes… she was why he was running.

B. continued to jog along, frissons of electric energy blitzing off of him like a force-field of sparks. His head was aching and he felt the throbbing in his loins like a hundred blacksmiths pounding their anvils. He swore again, thinking about how badly he wanted to find Mindy, take her back to his house, and make sweet, searing, raging love to her until she screamed out his name with breathless abandon… his *real* name. But that thought in itself caused a cold wave of nauseous fear to wash over him. He was terrified that she already knew too much; if she found out who he was, he was finished. Blinded by his haze of restless thoughts and immense sexual frustration, B. forged on, relieved when he caught sight of his beachfront condo building up ahead. Breathing hard, B. streaked up the street in the dark, finally ascending the steps to his building two at a time. He was completely unaware of anyone or anything else around him as the elevator carried him up to his penthouse. *Come on,* he groaned, knowing that he couldn't go without release much longer. In a matter of seconds, it would happen whether he was ready or not. Touching down at his floor, he pelted down the hall and crashed through the door to his condo.

Once he was inside, B. let out a sigh of relief. He now had the privacy to do what he needed to do. Taking a deep breath, he channeled the energy inside him until it was a column of searing electricity. He began to shimmer as he reached his hands upward, directing the column of energy up through his outstretched arms. As the energy surged through his body, B. felt the screaming ecstasy of a thousand orgasms as the current exploded into the atmosphere, causing him to disappear into the air, expanding into his alter form. It was only after it was too late that he looked over his shoulder and saw Mindy standing in the doorway, her mouth open in shock.

***

Astounded and shaking, Mindy leaned heavily against the doorframe and blinked several times to make sure she was awake. Completely baffled, she stared into the room where B.

had been standing just a moment ago. She had come to talk to him, ask him why he kept running from her. He left every time they began to get intimate, tearing away with the same urgent haste. She'd come to calm him down… and he'd shimmered and disappeared right before her eyes.

After a moment to get her bearings, or what she had left, Mindy stepped cautiously into the apartment and let the door close softly behind her. She knew it might be risky to stick around but she wanted to find out what happened.

"B.?" she called hesitantly, but the only sound was the soft ticking of the clock on the mantel. After a few minutes, when no additional cosmic blasts came, Mindy decided to take a look at where B. lived. Looking around, Mindy noticed that his quarters were very Spartan, with light gray carpet, white walls, and gray plaid drapes. There was a gray couch against the wall and a leather recliner parked near the large bay window, which ordinarily provided an exquisite view of Lake Champlain.

As she perused the living room, Mindy came to realize that B. had very little *stuff.* There were no sweaters thrown over chairs or DVDs on the floor. In fact, the only thing that caught Mindy's attention was the large bookcase against the other wall. Carefully, Mindy tiptoed over and began to page through his collection. The bookcase was bursting with titles on all topics imaginable, from classics to astrology to botany to astrophysics. B. had several thick math books as well as some very old books, perhaps collectors' editions. Picking one up, she saw that it was a tattered manuscript dated from 1804. *Wow, he really likes old things,* Mindy thought with a pensive frown, both intrigued and uneasy. She sat on the floor holding the book for several seconds, thinking. As she sat there, Mindy noticed something else odd about B.'s apartment, and that was a notable absence of any pictures of him or his family. Glancing up at the mantel, she noticed several pictures, but none of them were of people. Curious,

Mindy got up to take a closer look at the mysterious photographs. They were all natural scenes, presumably of the city, at different times of year. There was a shot of the city of Burlington in Indian summer, all its glory beaming through with a clear azure sky, golden sun glowing down on the buildings, tall, shady trees with deep green leaves and the calm waters of Lake Champlain at the foot of the photograph. Amazed, Mindy gently picked it up and studied it closer, noting the incredible artistic talent of the photographer. She could almost feel the warm sun on her back and the summer breeze whipping through her hair. Startled by the strange sensation, she set the photo down and looked over the others. There was Burlington in the tender buds of spring, the chill of winter still in the air, a bold and majestic autumn full of rich oranges, reds, yellows, and browns, and finally, a deep and powerful winter, the snow-capped city, polar wind strong enough to fell castles with its might. But despite the dreary weather, Christmas lights stalwartly lit the streets like a mighty lighthouse guiding wayward ships. Mindy was fascinated by the winter photograph, by the energy it exuded. Cautiously, she reached out to touch it gently. As her fingers made contact with the silver frame, Mindy was not prepared to feel the gust of icy wind and warmth of the Christmas lights all wrapped in one. The sensation was powerful and unusual, but what shocked her more than the polar chill were the strong currents of B.'s energy radiating out of the picture. Jerking her hand away, she stared at the beguiling photographs, wondering if she had finally gone absolutely insane. It was hard to explain, but it felt like the pictures were his, the pictures were him.

Finally, unable to come up with any coherent explanation, she shook her head and rubbed her eyes, walking towards the adjoining door. Peering through the crack in the door, she saw that it was B.'s bedroom. For a moment she felt an intimate sense of foreboding, like she shouldn't go into his bedchamber, but curious as always, Mindy creaked open the door anyway.

B.'s bedroom was like the living room, same gray carpet and gray draperies. His bed was an antique-looking structure with a black comforter. Looking at the bed, Mindy blushed hard. The covers were slightly rumpled and the faint scent of B. hung in the air. She pictured him as he slept on a hot summer night-- shirt off, brown hair rumpled, arms out to the side. She blushed even harder as she thought about sleeping next to him, flushed and satisfied, her black cocktail dress flung over a chair in the corner. His bedroom was bare except for a radio in the corner, and another stack of books in the corner. *Man, he's just about got a library in here,* Mindy mused. She knew he was intelligent, but she never expected a handy coffee-shop owner and landlord to have so many books. After a moment's wait, Mindy decided that she was going to stay and wait for B. to get back so that she could find out what was going on. Admittedly, she was a bit frightened, but she sort of hoped in the back of her mind that he was just a great magician or something. Regardless, she knew she wasn't going to leave without answers. Feeling lonely in the silent apartment, Mindy fixed herself a drink and picked a book from the bookshelf to read while she waited. But she only got through a few pages before exhaustion from the day overtook her and she sank back into B.'s soft bed, falling deeply asleep.

***

Mindy awoke slowly, aware only of the soft mattress beneath her and the cloak of darkness around her. She stirred faintly and blinked sleepily, still half-asleep. Suddenly, the soft sound of a door creaking open startled her out of her slumber. Her eyes flew open when a shadowy figure flicked the light switch and the room was flooded with light. Mindy struggled and squinted as she came out of her sleep, trying to remember where she was. Once her eyes adjusted, she realized that she was lying flat on her back on B.'s bed, and he was standing in the doorway.

"Oh, my god!" Mindy murmured, feeling mortified that she had fallen asleep on his bed. She burned red from embarrassment but also felt the heat of his gaze lingering on her as she sat up. When she looked up, she saw him standing there, his gray eyes stormy with emotion and the legs of his pants rolled up as if they had gotten wet. The air around him sparkled with invisible energy, though his force field was much more controlled than earlier. Mindy could do nothing but sit on the edge of his bed, gaping at him openmouthed. He was back! She had so many questions to ask him, so many answers that she needed. Why were his photographs magical? Where did he go when he disappeared? Who was he?

"Where did you go when you disappeared?" Mindy blurted, her voice breaking the silence of the room. She looked up pleadingly at B., who was still standing in the doorway, his hands in his pockets.

As soon as the question slipped into the air, B.'s shoulders stiffened and he looked at the floor. "I didn't go anywhere," he said softly. Moving out of the doorframe, he went to get his car keys off of the desk by the window. "It's getting late, Araminta." His voice was still soft and unwavering. "Let me drive you home."

"That's impossible," Mindy protested, pressing him further. "I looked for you and you were gone. I don't know what happened, but you disappeared before my eyes! What am I supposed to make of that?"

B. shrugged mildly. "I think you've had a lot to drink," he said calmly. "Would you like a glass of water?"

"I know what I saw," Mindy said softly. "I'm sorry, B., I just want an explanation. I won't say anything to anyone."

B.'s gray eyes flashed like a bolt of lightning and he set his keys down hard on the table. "Sometimes there are things in life that you will never understand," B. said coldly. He looked like he was struggling to keep his temper in check. "Now let me take you home."

Mindy glanced around, looking for a way to stall him. Her eyes landed on his photograph collection. "Your photographs are beautiful," she told him, hoping that she could maybe indirectly get some information out of him. "They seem to glow with the seasons. They're breathtaking."

"Thank you," B. replied shortly, shrugging his coat on. He didn't comment further.

"Before we go, may I see one of them?" Mindy asked pleadingly, searching his stony face.

B. remained silent for several minutes. "If you must," he said finally. He reached up onto the shelf and took down the summer picture. Then, he crossed the room and handed it to Mindy.

Even though he was still cold of demeanor, Mindy felt the air begin to tingle with feverish, magnetic energy and her heart beat faster with anticipation as he came closer. Despite his attempt to remain stoic, Mindy felt the heat radiating off of him and saw the warring emotions flickering deep in his eyes. As their fingers brushed, a jolt of raw electricity shot up Mindy's arm and she gasped softly, her lips parting as she looked up into his eyes. She just wanted to keep touching him, forever. "It's so beautiful," she repeated. As she studied the photo, she became aware of a new sensation. There was a faint, strange scent in the air, one that she couldn't place. It seemed to be on B.'s clothes. She sniffed the air and studied him, trying to figure it out. Slowly, Mindy figured out that it wasn't just one scent, but many scents in one. The first one she became aware of was the scent of the coffee shop, Arabica and glazed donuts. But as she delved deeper, she found other scents slowly unfolding and revolving, like the petals of a flower.

"What are you doing?" B. wondered, his brow furrowed in confusion.

"Oh, I just wondered what that interesting smell is," she commented. "You didn't smell like that at the beach."

"I don't smell anything," B. said with a quick shrug. "Would you like to see my book collection?"

B. moved away to go grab a stack of books and Mindy found herself fighting to concentrate on the scent. He returned and began jabbering away about British and American history, clearly trying to distract her.

But even as his voice drilled through her thoughts, shattering them, the scents kept coming, clearer and stronger, the accompanying picture flashing through Mindy's head. Mindy smelled the fresh breeze off of the lake, the scent of the town bakery. Next, Mindy caught a whiff of the midday heat of traffic, the toothpastey smell of the dentist's office. In her mind she saw the clothing boutique, the library, the church, the flower garden, one place after another as the scent became apparent. As she struggled to figure it out, B. talked louder, shoving more books under her nose.

"That's very interesting," she said finally, gently pushing away the book on the Revolutionary War. "But that smell, it's like the entire city at once. The bakery. The coffee shop. The flower garden. The marina. I don't know where you could have gone."

B. turned away with the book in his hand. "Good God, Araminta, will you just drop it?" he fumed. He set the book down and whirled to face her. "What do you want with a guy like me anyway?" he challenged her, throwing up his hands. His gaze bored hard into hers and she saw anger, hurt and fear in his eyes.

"Just listen to me," Mindy pleaded, putting her hand gently on his shoulder. "I've never met anyone like you. You... I just can't even describe how you make me feel. I like what I see and want to know more of you."

B. shook his head, a wounded look in his eyes. His resolve seemed to be weakening. "I like you too, Araminta," he said softly. "But I don't think it will work."

Mindy ran her hands over his stiff shoulders, feeling torn apart by the sadness and fear she saw in his eyes. "Just tell me one thing," she whispered. "What does B. stand for?"

B.'s resolve seemed to crumble completely and he sighed heavily. His eyes were still veiled and he said nothing, staring at the floor. His jaw was clenched and his hands were in fists at his sides. As Mindy looked around the apartment; the pieces finally started coming together. The smell of him, all the scents were places around the city. His apartment was full of pictures of the city in various seasons. The way he talked about city history as if he was there. His name, B. Fairmont, sounded like Vermont. "Burlington," Mindy whispered softly as the new revelation washed over her. "Burlington, Vermont."

B. gasped and jerked away as if he'd been burned. Judging from the wild look of panic in his eyes, Mindy knew that she was right about his name. Mindy stood, rooted in place, trying to figure out what it meant. "I don't understand," she said slowly. "It's like you *are* the city of Burlington. But how can that be?"

B. turned away, still cold and unresponsive, fists clenched, struggling for control. He flickered briefly before Mindy's eyes, appearing as the city, before he returned to his disgruntled human form.

Mindy didn't know what to say to him, how to deal with the supernatural revelation. But she didn't have to say anything, because B. abruptly strode into his bedroom and slammed the door so hard that it rattled the windows.

Chapter Eighteen

The next morning, Mindy awoke feeling like she was swimming weightlessly in a deep well, floating aimlessly but struggling to find her path. It was still dark outside, and the waning rays of moonlight shone in ethereally through the crack in the curtains. Still feeling weightless and confused, Mindy rolled out of bed and glided to the window, as if drawn by some magnetic force. Silently, she parted the curtains and gazed out over the darkened city. Stars twinkled mysteriously in the sky above and the moon cast its final rays over the shadowy buildings below. The streets were quiet, with only a few early-morning commuters. Even though the window was closed, Mindy could feel the foggy chill in the air. Through the slight haze, the traffic lights on the hill still steadily, sleepily changed from green to yellow to red and back. Mindy was amazed by the beauty of the morning, and she felt B.'s energy shimmering in the air, softly, as if he were still asleep.

Deep in thought, Mindy continued to stare out the window, thinking about what had happened the night before. She had followed B. back from the gala to make sure he was okay, and to find out why he kept running from her. She knew that he had a secret, but she never imagined that the scope of his identity would be so grand. Thinking back on it, Mindy saw how the clues had begun to add up: his name, the strange, beautiful energy that always shimmered around him, how he had built the Manor House, talked about the past like he was there and had the mysterious photographs in his condo.

Still, it was a lot for Mindy to get used to. He *was* Burlington, Vermont. She had heard talk of "falling in love" with a city before, but ever since she had touched down in Burlington, her reality had been infused with magic and changed forever. *I guess this is how it is,* she thought.

She had a choice to make. She could go back to dreary, lifeless New Jersey, running away from a concept she couldn't fathom; or she could stay and try to make something out of what she had. Out on the horizon, the sun was just beginning to come up, casting the city in a beautiful, muted lavender glow with pink streaks across the sky and calm, still reflections dancing over the surface of Lake Champlain. *So beautiful,* Mindy murmured, putting her hand on the windowsill. *I wouldn't dream of leaving.*

Suddenly, Mindy's silent reflections were interrupted by the ringing of her cell phone. Startled, Mindy tore away from the window and rooted around in her purse, wondering who the hell was calling her at this ridiculous hour.

"Hello?" Mindy mumbled into the phone.

"Hey, Miss America," Troy Haverman's loud, obnoxious voice rolled through the speakers. "I'll be waiting for you at the airport in fifteen minutes. I'll carry your luggage if you let me squeeze your ass."

Mindy exhaled through her nose. "That won't be necessary," she said stiffly. "I'm not going back."

Troy laughed, a harsh, mocking sound. "Yeah, right. You'll come back as soon as I can talk to Carrera. She likes me a lot, you know. I've seen her checking out my basket."

"If you're so confident, have me transferred," Mindy said disdainfully, ignoring his lewd comment.

Troy simply laughed again and there was a *click* as the line was transferred to Catherine Carrera's office.

"Catherine Carrera speaking," the Hispanic woman's curt, businesslike voice cut through the phone line.

"Hi, this is Mindy Cullen," Mindy explained. "I was supposed to be back today but some very important business has come up and I must stay for at least a week and a half. I'll take leave without pay."

Ms. Carrera listened for several moments, saying nothing. Finally, she responded. "Very well, Mindy, though I'll warn you that it isn't a wise career decision."

Mindy took a breath. "I'm aware of that," she replied. "But it's very important to me. Thanks for understanding."

When Mindy had finished talking to the manager, she set her phone down and let out a light sigh. She had taken care of work, but she still had no idea what to do with B. *I want to at least give him a chance,* she thought as she looked out at the rising sun. Though it looked like it would be a nice day, there was a cold mist in the atmosphere that chilled Mindy to the bone. It was more than a physical chill, Mindy felt B. pulling away from her, shrouding himself in a wintry cloak. No doubt had she shocked and perhaps frightened him last night when she had uncovered his identity.

It's okay, Mindy whispered as she gazed out over the amorphous, rolling hills and still waters of Lake Champlain beneath the dishwater-mauve sky. *Your secret is always safe with me.*

As the day dawned, the sun went behind clouds and a moody, desolate lake breeze kicked up, whipping across the landscape and hurling handfuls of leaves into the air. There was no rain, but Mindy sensed that B. was restless, withdrawn. *I have to go to him,* she thought, devastated by how empty she felt without his presence. She showered and dressed, donning her black sweater and yoga pants, since it felt like deep winter outside. Then, she headed to her car, not quite sure where she was going. She drove past the Manor House, hoping that the delicious aromas and warm atmosphere would make her feel better. But when she saw that B. was nowhere in sight, she simply drove on, deciding to pick up some groceries, do her laundry, and think about how to get out of the mess she was in.

***

It was about 5:00 PM, and the weather had gotten progressively worse throughout the day. Mindy was sitting on the couch in her hotel room, worn down from her errands and missing B. All day long, she had wandered the streets like a pleading ghost, an outsider. Now, after the entire day, it was beginning to wear her down. She shivered and wrapped herself in a plaid afghan as she stared out at the sheets of pouring rain blanketing the windows. *Maybe this was a mistake,* she thought mournfully. *Maybe I should just go home.* She rose off the couch and headed into the kitchenette to brew herself some tea, anything to fight off the bone-jarring chill. She planned to just drink a few glasses of wine, sleep the rest of the day away, and plan to fly home in the morning. *I'm gonna need a lot of wine to forget him,* she thought.

But when she opened the refrigerator, a bag of apples caught her eye. Mindy remembered a friend saying once that no man could resist an apple pie. At the time, Mindy had laughed and said that it was silly to put that much effort into a man. But now, she picked up the bag of apples and set it on the counter, staring at it as if her life depended on it. She needed a way to show him that she was sincere, to tame his defenses. And if he was like any other man, food would do the trick. *This is my last shot,* Mindy thought, her energy renewed as she pulled out a mixing bowl and some utensils. As she worked, she listened to a sad ballad on the radio and watched the rain come down outside. She imagined sailing on a rugged sea amidst a roiling storm, clinging to the mast with all her might. *I won't give up the ship,* she whispered.

Set with determination, Mindy pulled a nearly-perfect apple pie from the oven thirty minutes later. She set it on a rack to cool and headed into her bedroom to change her clothes. Rooting through her suitcase, she found a silky dark gray cocktail dress that she had brought. She realized that she could have worn it to the beach gala, but it was more fun to buy a new one. No doubt her gray dress was well-worn, but it would have to do. Mindy put on her dress, nylons, and heels, and pulled her hair up into a pretty hairclip. Looking in the mirror, she decided that she looked pretty good. The dress flowed over her slim frame, clinging in all the right places. She fastened in silver hoop earrings and sealed her lips with gloss. Even though she was beautiful, she could see in her own eyes the pain that something was missing. She dabbed her eyes and turned away, unable to look at her reflection any longer. Checking the clock, she pursed her lips and shrugged on her hooded jacket, hoping that the rain would abate long enough for her to get to B.'s condo. It was dark and blustery outside, but Mindy couldn't tell whether the rain had stopped. She grabbed a bottle of white wine she had bought and tucked it under her arm, picking up the pie in a bag as well. Then, silently, she left her hotel room with one light on and locked the door, riding the elevator down to the main floor.

"Say, Miss Mindy, where you going in this awful weather?" she saw her friend Ernest cheerfully crossing the lobby toward her.

"I need to go see a friend," Mindy explained. "It's important."

Ernest gave her a sympathetic look and moved to the door to open it. "Well, don't catch cold," he told her. "It's pretty blustery out there."

Mindy thanked him and stepped out into the cold, dark night, shivering as she was slapped in the face by an icy gust of wind. Luckily, the pouring rain had dwindled to a weepy mist that shrouded the air. Mindy hurried toward her car, her heels clicking along on the wet pavement. Fumbling for her keys, she managed to open the car door and get in, safely depositing the pie on the seat beside her. Once she was in her car, she turned up the heater and the radio to provide some comfort on the drive over to B.'s condo.

Shivering from the cold and humming with apprehensive anticipation, Mindy gripped the wheel white-knuckled as she drove through the rain-slicked streets, her wipers dislodging clumps of wet leaves from her windshield. She swished through puddles and bumps in the road as she drove down to the lakefront neighborhood where B.'s condo was. Looking out at the lake, she saw that it was choppy and restless, and B.'s condo building stood forebodingly in front of her, as if daring her to enter. Mindy parked her car and got out as close to the door as possible, clutching her gifts as she ascended the steps.

As she rode up in the elevator and walked down the carpeted hallway towards B.'s door, her apprehension increased along with the urge to go forward. *I must go to him,* Mindy thought, finding herself drawn closer to that white door with every step. Her heart was pounding erratically as she stopped in front of the door and her hand was badly shaking when she lifted it to knock. Would he be there? Would he send her away? The questions were racing in her mind, but Mindy knocked anyway.

The world fell silent and time was frozen as Mindy waited for B. to come to the door. There was nothing but immense quiet at first, but then, she heard the soft fumbling of the lock being turned back, and suddenly, the door swung open.

Mindy sucked in a deep breath and she was paralyzed as she laid eyes on B. Even though he looked a bit fatigued, he was the most beautiful thing she had ever seen. *Oh, my,* she breathed involuntarily as she looked him over. His hair was rumpled and he was dressed in his Vermont shirt and jeans, his feet clad only in socks. His sleeves were rolled up, showing the tattoos winding around his brawny arms, and he was leaning against the doorway. He was looking down, his eyes veiled with barren winter, and beneath the coldness, she could sense a deep, liquid wound in his soul. Finally, after several moments, B. lifted his gaze and looked Mindy over, his expression nearly tearing her in two.

"What are you doing here?" he murmured softly, brokenly.

"I came to talk to you," Mindy's own voice was shaky, and she held out the pie. "And tell you I'm sorry."

B. responded by turning away and starting to close the door.

"B., wait!" Mindy pleaded, pushing open the door. "Just let me talk to you. Then I'll go."

Reluctantly, B. relented and held the door open, padding across the room as she followed him in. Mindy shut the door behind them and set the pie on the desk. She noticed that B.'s apartment was mostly darkened except for a dim light in the corner. He was standing at the window, his hands in his pockets, his gaze faraway.

"You don't have to be afraid," Mindy began softly. "I know you didn't want me to find out, but your secret will always be safe."

B. tensed and shrugged his shoulders. "What's done is done," he murmured, starting to turn away again.

Mindy knew that this was getting her nowhere. Shedding her coat, she moved towards him in her dress, softly switching on the radio. Surprisingly, the same song was playing that they had danced to in the coffee shop. He must have been thinking about her.

When she was close to B., she leaned in to whisper in his ear. "There is something else I want to tell you," she murmured, stroking her hands over his stiff shoulders. "I came here because I want to be with you. Just you."

B.'s expression remained unreadable but Mindy could feel him beginning to sway to the music, gaze still glued to the floor. Slowly, sensually, she ran her hands up and down his arms, softly squeezing his biceps. "You're so beautiful," she whispered, and she felt him suck in a sharp breath as her lips followed her hands, and she began to trail a soft line of kisses along his neck. He stood still, his breath becoming heavy, and Mindy could feel the heat radiating off of him as she touched every inch of him. She had never seduced a man before, but the scent of him was strong and husky in the air and as Mindy ran her hands over him, she felt the steely heat of his erection pressing against her. Cautiously, curiously, she reached down and cupped the hot bulge in her hands. B. let out a strangled groan and drew her in for a kiss, their tongues tangling in a sweet, tortured, passionate dance. As they kissed, Mindy continued to stroke him, causing his passion to become more intense. He gripped her hips in his strong hands and held her against him as they spun around the room. The tables were turned and Mindy cried out softly as his erection ground against her in just the right place. She reached up and looped her arms around his neck, kissing him with fervor. Their dance grew reckless and fiery, electricity burning in B.'s veiled eyes as he crushed Mindy against him and let his hot hands explore her skin through the silk of her dress. Mindy blushed as he reached up under her skirt and tore away her pantyhose. She helped by stepping out of them and moaned as B. held her in his work-worn hands, thrusting his fingers inside her. He gave a husky murmur when he found her already wet for him.

"God, B., don't stop," she breathed, closing her eyes as his fingers massaged her most intimate place.

"Look at me, Araminta," she heard his soft, commanding voice near her ear. Saturated with pleasure, she opened her eyes and another flood of arousal shot through her when she saw the veiled hunger burning in his eyes. She rocked harder into his hand as she felt the throes of orgasm begin to creep upon her. "This time say my real name, Araminta," he murmured, thrust his fingers into her one more time, with a twist.

At this, she came apart in his arms, gasping. "Burlington," she murmured. "That was wonderful."

They pulled apart, and they gazed at each other with luminous eyes. "Next time I want to be inside you," B. murmured, searching her eyes. "Will you let me?"

Mindy looked at him lovingly and trailed her fingers over the side of his face. "Yes, Burlington," she whispered. "Yes."

No sooner had she said that that he pushed her back on the bed, covering her with his hot, hard frame. Gently, he parted her legs and slid inside her, and she murmured with discomfort as she adjusted to the size of him. The discomfort was soon obliterated and Mindy's senses were overwhelmed as he began to move on her, his breath rasping softly against her face. She gripped his strong biceps and tilted her head back, sighing in pleasure as he slowly rocked into her, her entire world consumed in the scent of him, the essence of him. Soon, the sparks caught fire and the pace of their passion became frenetic, with oaths, gasps, scraping of lips and nails against flesh. At the fever pitch, Mindy's whole universe exploded before her eyes and she screamed out his name, bucking under him and spiraling through the cosmos. Her voice fused with his as he, too, groaned his release, spilling his hot flush within her.

Looking out the window, Mindy saw the trailing beams of a shooting star fading into the dark night. "Did you do that?" she asked softly, amazed.

B. blushed and shrugged. "It happens sometimes, I guess. If I'm not careful, my feelings manifest in the weather. That's being a city, I guess."

Mindy looked him on with wonder. "So, the pleading, passionate summers, and deep barren winters, they are all created by you?"

B. shrugged again. "Somewhat," he answered. "But only for this region. I do have to follow natural law, though. I can't make it snow in July, at least not ordinarily."

Mindy processed this, thinking of all the photographs of different seasons that he had in the living room. She had no words, but simply traced the tattoo on his arm with the tips of her fingers. "You're beautiful," she whispered again, more to herself than to him.

They lay there for a few moments in silence, until B. sat up in bed. "Are you hungry for some of that pie?" he asked.

Mindy laughed. "Come to think of it, I am," she replied, kissing him softly. "But we'd better be back here when we're done."

B. made a sound low in his throat. "We will be," he murmured, streaking his hot hands up her sides to cup her breasts. "But you'd better stop if you want any pie."

Chapter Nineteen

The next morning, Mindy was comfortably stretched out beneath the blankets, eyes closed, brown hair spread out across her pillow. Slowly, the light of dawn began to infiltrate the starry night sky, and Mindy stirred as the cusp of daylight peeked in the window. With a pleasant sigh, she rolled over, slowly waking up. Looking around, she realized that she was in B.'s bedroom. A soft smile came to her lips as she recalled their long night of making love. She had come to apologize and ended up seducing him. She sighed again as she remembered how his reserve had weakened and the fire burned bright in his gray eyes. She had started out as the seductress, but then the tables had been turned, and he ended up blowing her entire world to smithereens of stardust, his touch leaving her breathless. She was saturated in him, his presence, and even her bare skin smelled like him. She loved it.

Speaking of which, Mindy thought, glancing over at the rumpled covers beside her. B. wasn't there, but Mindy caught the aroma of fresh-brewed dark coffee emanating from the kitchen and heard the steady hiss of the coffee maker. As he read her thoughts, the door softly swung open and B. stepped in.

"Good morning," he said quietly, giving her his signature half-smile. Mindy looked up and let her gaze wander over him, taking in all his glory. He looked fresh as the sunrise, and Mindy could feel the rays of sun sparkling softly around him. His brown hair was slightly rumpled, and he was wearing rolled-up jeans and a dark gray t-shirt that accented his eyes and showed off his tattoos. He looked strong and relaxed, and Mindy could sense in him the power of the seasons; the beauty of Indian summer, the torrential winds of winter, the strength of steel bridges, it was all there and radiating off of him in subtle waves. Mindy couldn't help but to stare in wonder, a smile spreading on her face.

B.'s eyes darkened with passion and he fixed his intense gaze on Mindy when he noticed her studying him. "Like what you see, Araminta?" he murmured teasingly, gliding closer to the bed.

Mindy blushed. "Yes," she whispered, looking up into his stormy gray eyes.

With his gaze still locked on hers, B. bent and slowly peeled the covers away as if he were unwrapping a present. Mindy's blush intensified as the covers slid lower, revealing inch after inch of her bare, alabaster skin. It was one thing to be naked in bed at night, when it was dark, but being laid bare in the light of the morning was almost too intense for Mindy to take. B.'s gaze was like a thousand sunbeams, burning its way up and down her skin. His breath became heavy as he slid his hands up her sides, taking her breasts in his hands. He murmured softly, his eyes burning with liquid fire as he squeezed, learning her shape.

"Oh, my, B.," Mindy murmured as she arched her back, reaching up to loop her arms around his neck. She flipped her hair out of the way and leaned in for a gentle kiss, her hands resting on his strong shoulders. The kiss was at first slow and sweet, and B. peeled his shirt over his head, tossing it aside.

In the light of the morning sun, Mindy was in awe of his physique, so earthy and entirely male. Carefully, she trailed her palms over his chest and back up again, and then explored his arms. It wasn't just his body that she found amazing; Mindy wanted to show her reverence for this amazing man in any way she could.

"Lay back, Burlington," Mindy whispered in his ear, trailing her lips along his jawline. "I want to touch every inch of you."

B. leaned back on the bed, studying her with his light gray eyes. "I won't argue with that," he murmured with a smile, but his gaze was veiled with fire.

"I've been wanting to do this since I first met you," Mindy confessed softly as she helped rid him of the rest of his clothes. Finally, he lay naked and gleaming before her, and his cheeks seemed to flush slightly as she smiled at him. Softly, she lowered her lips to his shoulder and traced her tongue around the tattoo on his arm. "You're so beautiful," she whispered.

B. closed his eyes and clung to her as she kept her promise to touch every inch of him. He stiffened and let out a soft gasp when she touched him where it mattered the most, and stroked her hair as she replaced her hands with her tongue.

Mindy loved the power she had over him, the pleasure she was giving him, and his soft groans of approval. When she finally pulled away, his breathing was ragged and he was burning with heat. "Enough, Araminta," he groaned, forcefully spreading her legs and pulling her down on top of him. Mindy sucked in a breath as he filled her, thrusting open the places that were still tender from the night before. Slowly, the pain morphed into phantom pleasure, and Mindy moved with him, letting him take her hard. When their insatiable desire flamed out at the core, she surrendered to him with a gasp of his name. Outside, the sun seemed to burn brighter as they climaxed.

"I can see why you don't want your secret spread around," Mindy teased him, gesturing out the window. "You'd have no privacy in your sex life."

B. laughed and playfully smacked her bottom. "Be quiet." But then his face became serious as he rose to get dressed. "Seriously, though," he said soberly, pulling his shirt over his head. His eyes were faraway. "Aren't you even a little bit freaked out that I am Burlington, Vermont?"

Mindy sat up and covered herself with a towel. "I was surprised," she replied softly. "Amazed. Maybe confused. But never freaked out." She put her hand on his arm. "Every time I look at you, I just want to know your story, yourself. Tell me everything."

B. seemed to relent slightly, his shoulders relaxing. "Well, join me in the kitchen, then," he requested. "I made coffee."

In a few minutes, Mindy had showered and dressed. She was lucky enough to have a set of extra clothes in her bag. The weather was more temperate today than it had been, so the long-sleeved navy blue shirt and taupe shorts were perfect. Mindy dried her hair and twisted it up in a bun, and made her way into the kitchen where B. was sitting at the table. She stopped in the doorway and studied him. He had his back to her and appeared to be looking out the picture window over the lake, deep in thought. He had his coffee cup in his hand and his gaze was faraway, unreadable. Silently, Mindy crossed the room and put her hand on his shoulder. "Hey," she said softly.

B. turned and looked up at her, his eyes full of solemn, intense wisdom. "Araminta," he murmured. "I left some coffee for you."

Mindy poured herself a cup and joined him at the table. "Tell me about you, Burlington," she said once she had seated herself across from him.

He took a sip of his coffee and regarded her languidly. "What do you want to know about me?" he wondered.

"Everything, actually," Mindy said quietly. "But how come you're only my age if the city's been around for hundreds of years?"

"It happens this way," B. replied, reaching for a cookie on a platter that he had put out. "Ever since I was founded, I start around human age twenty and cycle up to fifty or sixty. Then, I reappear at twenty again, erasing everyone's memory of me."

"Wow," Mindy breathed. "So, will I forget you in thirty years?"

B. shook his head, looking down. "You know who I really am," he said flatly. His expression was unreadable, and he seemed tense. "Those who know my true identity never forget me."

"I'd never want to forget you," Mindy murmured, touching his hand across the table. "My whole life, I never loved a man. Until I met you. Please trust me."

"Who else knows who you really are?" Mindy whispered, searching his face.

"No one," B. said flatly, his eyes flashing. "And I hope it stays that way."

Mindy wondered if her questions were bothering him. "Don't worry," she murmured, taking both of his hands in hers. His hands were still at first but then he held on as well. "Take me around your city today," she requested, bringing his hand to her lips. "I want to see everything."

B. sat for several moments before a smile started to bloom on his face. "I'd love to," he said finally, his gray eyes shining softly. "No one has ever been this interested in me before."

Mindy smiled fondly at him and gently let his hands go. "Can I make you anything for breakfast?" she wondered, going to the refrigerator.

B. laughed. "I doubt you'll find much," he explained. "I don't spend a lot of time here in my human form."

Mindy opened the fridge and saw a bag of apples, a carton of milk, and a loaf of bread. "Wow, you're right," she agreed. She looked at him curiously. "I hope you don't mind me asking, but what happens to your body when you aren't in human form?"

B. smiled at her. "It's okay," he assured her. "I have the ability to channel myself into any form I wish. The only ones I use are my human form or the entire city at once."

"Is your human personality like your city one?" Mindy wondered. "I mean, are you still the same person?"

B. nodded. "I am who I am," he answered modestly. "I have thoughts and feelings, likes and dislikes, good days and bad. Whether I'm looking over the city or through these eyes, I'm the same."

Mindy was gazing at him with rapt fascination, touched deeply by his impassioned truth. "You're so beautiful," she said softly. "In any form."

"Araminta," he murmured, sweeping her into his strong arms and crushing his lips to hers. Mindy's entire world was set ablaze as the taste of him flooded her mouth, and the smell of Arabica beans and Indian summer surrounded her like a cloud. Behind her closed eyes, she could see in him every season, past and present. The pictures were really more of a sense, but they were beautiful. Mindy gasped in awe and pleasure, both at the lovely sights and the heavenly feel of his lips on hers. She felt herself becoming once again immensely aroused, and she melted into him with a breathy plea, giving him everything she had. The kiss quickly spiraled out of control, and B. shoved his work-worn fingers inside her, bringing her to yet another climax at his hands. Mindy writhed against his hand, oblivious to everything except the searing flames that engulfed her world. Opening her eyes, she was met with B.'s blazing gaze as he touched all of the spots that were already sensitive. Finally, feeling like she would burst, she let the flames take her and breathed his name, rewarded by the sharp spark in his eyes.

When they pulled apart, B. gave her a lazy smile. "I have half a mind to just stay here and make love to you all day," he pointed out.

Mindy slung her arm around his shoulders. "We have all night," she replied. "I don't know about you, but I could use some breakfast. What's your best restaurant?"

"My favorite is the Manor House," he said, picking up his car keys. "Let's go."

Together, they left the penthouse arm-in-arm and rode the elevator down to the ground floor. As they stepped outside, Mindy was met with a gust of fresh, sweet autumn mountain air. In the distance, the mountains were turning shades of red and orange as the trees began to lose their leaves. The sun was sparkling in a cloudless sky and soft waves lapped at the shore of Lake Champlain's deep blue waters.

Mindy turned and looked up at B. with a smile. "At least I know you're in a good mood today," she teased him. "It's a beautiful day."

B. chuckled. "You're right about both of those things," he replied. "But I don't want you thinking I'm in a bad mood every time it rains. After all, I need to keep the land watered."

"Right," Mindy answered as they got into his truck. "So there's good mood rain and bad mood rain?"

B. nodded as he started the motor. "Absolutely," he confirmed with a smile. "Believe me, you'll know the difference."

As they rode over to the Manor House, Mindy watched the beautiful scenery pass by the windows, all of it uniquely

Burlington. "Tell me something," Mindy said quietly as they drove along, the radio playing softly. "I know this sounds silly, but do you have parents or a family? Did you grow up or were you always like this?"

B. turned to look at her. "That's not a silly question at all," he responded. "And I never had a mother and father if that's what you're wondering," he paused. "But the closest to family were my founding fathers, the men who designated and named me as Burlington, Vermont. They helped me get started and cared about me very much. And as far as growing up, I started out as a young, fledgling city and I continue to grow and change every day."

"But your founding fathers died hundreds of years ago," Mindy pointed out. "Don't you ever get lonely?"

B. shrugged. "Sometimes," he answered. "It's generally a pretty solitary job. But that's improved greatly since I met you."

Mindy blushed. "I hope so," she murmured. "I never want you to be lonely."

They finished their conversation just as they pulled up at the Manor House. "Do you want to go in?" B. asked. "Or would you rather eat outside somewhere?"

Mindy glanced out at the beautiful sunshine. "Let's go outside," she suggested. "I want you to show me around."

They pulled up at the drive-thru window and the guy on duty reached out to bump fists with B. "Hey, boss," he grinned. "Skipping work today?"

B. chuckled. "It's my business, I can skip work if I want," he said with a laugh. "I'd like a cinnamon latte and a dark roast, please. Also, get us two slices of pumpkin pie with whipped cream."

The guy prepared their coffee and food and handed it out the window. "Have fun on your daaate," he sang out.

"Get back to work, Greg," B. called with mock sternness as they drove away.

"Pumpkin pie for breakfast?" Mindy teased, smiling at B as she took a delicious spoonful. "You're very health-conscious this morning."

"Don't criticize me, Araminta, you know you like it," he countered, smiling as well. He gave her a knowing look and she flushed deep red, gathering that he wasn't just talking about the pie.

After their unbalanced but delicious breakfast on the road, Mindy and B. got out to walk around. B. showed her his oldest streets, explaining the history of the Church Street Marketplace. As she looked around, her hand clasped in his, Mindy could see how B. had turned from a fiery, energetic young city into a stately, wise one. They talked about the buildings and Mindy was surprised to hear that B. had helped build many of them. Mindy got a starry look in her eyes as she imagined him working hard, hammering ancient wood in place, his chest bare in the afternoon sun.

B. must have picked up on her train of thought because he chuckled. "I didn't do it just to impress the ladies, if that's what you think," he teased her. "In all seriousness, I have a responsibility to my people and I wanted to make sure everything was done right."

"You do a good job," Mindy told him. "What happens if you don't like the way the mayor is handling things?" she wondered.

B. gave her a sideways smile. "I can be very influential," he murmured.

"I've always enjoyed the privilege to vote," Mindy commented as they walked along. "I'm a strong Democrat."

"I couldn't agree more," B. answered. "After all, these are the people who are running the government. And, yes, I'm a Democrat too." He smiled at her, his eyes alive with light. "I've seen a lot in my couple hundred years. Government can be flawed, but it is very necessary."

Mindy grinned back at him and leaned her head on his shoulder. She loved how cultured and informed he was about everything. "You're so wise, Burlington," she said softly.

He put a finger to her lips. "B. In public I'm just B."

Mindy squeezed his hand. "Yeah, I know who you are," she said fondly.

A few hours later, they had finished walking around the city and were taking a break. "Take me down to the beach," Mindy said wistfully.

"I'd love to," B. agreed. "Let's walk. It will take a few minutes, but I'll point out things on the way."

The two of them gradually walked down the hilly slope of the city towards the beach, with B. pointing out sights along the way. He talked about almost every building, explaining parts of his history, things that Mindy never would have learned on an ordinary tour. He pointed out certain buildings, talking about how it was to build them or what materials they used. As they neared the marina, B. told Mindy about how things were shipped and ferried across the lake.

Finally, after several minutes of walking, they reached the shore and decided to sit on the pier. "It's been such a wonderful day," Mindy sighed, letting the lake breeze ruffle through her hair.

B. took his sneakers off and sloshed his bare feet in the water, looking pensive. "Indeed it has," he said softly, his gaze fixed on a sailboat on the horizon.

Mindy took in the sight of him, enchanted. The afternoon sun was turning his skin a golden shade, making his already handsome figure even more handsome. The lake breeze was blowing through his hair and around him, and he seemed to shimmer along with it. Looking at him again, Mindy found it fascinating how he seemed one with nature. It was hard to tell where he ended and the wind began, he seemed to flow with the wind. It was hard to tell whether the sun was shining on his skin or if he was glowing mystically from within.

After several moments, B. had still not spoken, so Mindy followed the direction of his gaze. Strangely, he seemed fixated on the blue, red, and orange striped sailboat, watching it as it floated along. "That's a pretty sailboat," Mindy commented.

B. barely nodded, still watching it. Mindy saw something in his eyes that looked like yearning.

"Do you like to go sailing?" she asked him.

He turned to her, his expression still troubled. "Never have," he replied softly. "Never will. I can't."

Mindy looked concerned. "Why not?" she wondered.

B. shrugged. "I'm the city's life force," he responded. "I can't leave the Greater Burlington area. I'll never know what it feels like to sail, fly, or see the other side of the shore. It's just in my rules."

"How do you feel about that?" Mindy said gently. "Does it bother you?"

B. shrugged again, squinting into the afternoon sun. "Most of the time not," he explained. "I don't really care about travelling. I would love to be able to take a boat, though. It's just one of those things I can't do."

Mindy leaned against his shoulder. "If it's too upsetting to watch the sailboats, we can go somewhere else."

B. shook his head. "It's fine. Besides, I like this time of day. The sun will be setting soon," he looked at his watch and turned to Mindy. "Let me show you something," he murmured in her ear.

Mindy waited and watched as B.'s hands began to glow almost brighter than the sun. Still, there was enough light that it wasn't too conspicuous. Mindy felt the change in the air as B. closed his eyes, shimmering with energy. Gradually, the sky began to turn a majestic color, sort of robin's-egg blue with the tops of the bare trees tinged red as if someone had spray-painted them. Then, some hints of cotton-candy pink crept into the fluffy white clouds. It looked almost like a painting, and Mindy turned to B. in awe and disbelief. "Did you just do that?" she breathed. "You're incredible."

B. shrugged and a faint blush crept into his cheeks. "I can't do much in my human form, especially out here in public," he explained. "Sometime I'll show you what I can do in city form. That's when I can really play with the weather."

Mindy watched the sky until the picture slowly faded away into a more ordinary late-afternoon scene. Suddenly, she realized that she hadn't eaten since lunch. "I could really use some dinner," she suggested to B.

B. smiled. "Dinner sounds great. I have a great place picked out." He winked at her, resting his hot hands on her shoulders. "And I have an even better place for after dinner."

Mindy shivered under his touch. "You're such a typical man," she murmured, her breath hitching as he grazed her shoulder blades with his thumbs. "And I love it."

B. grinned good-naturedly as they headed back, knowing he had won.

Chapter Twenty

The rest of the week flew by in such a state of idyllic paradise that Mindy was oblivious to anything but B. She spent the days with him, learning about parts of the city that she never knew existed. He took her to the abandoned railroad car, a quaint little park with ivy-covered trees, and many more quirky little places. Mindy found the revealing of these spots to be quite intimate, and was thrilled that B. would share them with her. Like a flower, Mindy opened to B. as well, giving him everything. She told him about her past, gave him her hopes and dreams. The two of them would stroll the sunny autumn days together, and then fill the cold nights with hot, searing passion. They often made love for hours upon hours, until Mindy felt like B. had permanently become a part of her. And when B. was in city form, he painted pretty skies for Mindy and reassured her with the swirling, gentle wind that he was near.

It was Friday morning, and Mindy was sitting in her room, staring pensively out the window. Suddenly, it began to dawn on her that eventually she would have to leave, and that she hadn't told B. when she would go. With a frown, she checked her email and found a warning message from the manager that this was one full week without pay. *What am I going to do?* Mindy fretted to herself. She knew that she couldn't just keep staying in the hotel, renting a car, and living in Vermont forever. Already, she checked her bank account and her money was beginning to run dangerously low. *And worst of all, it's not like B. could come visit,* Mindy thought. *He's stuck where he is. And I won't be able to afford a vacation like this for a while…*

The thought of being separated from B. made tears come to Mindy's eyes. *I love him,* she thought. *And I never want to leave him.* With a heavy heart, Mindy realized she had a choice to make. She could go back now while she still had money left, or she could stay another week without pay and risk going into debt. Looking out the window, Mindy saw her rental car in the lot and realized that she could take it back today. For the time being, Mindy decided that she would hold off on making any plan to stay or go back.

Mindy went about her day, took the rental car back, and stopped at the Manor House for lunch by taxi. B. was working in the morning and afternoon, so Mindy hung out for a while and sipped her coffee while she watched him work. She watched the way his eyes sparkled, the way he tossed his hair to the side, the straining of his muscles when he lifted the heavy bin of dirty dishes. B. had told Mindy that he did most of the repairs himself, and could do electric, plumbing, carpentry and roofing. Even though they weren't directly speaking, Mindy was content to just sit back and look at the man she loved. Every once in a while, B. would lift his gaze and a special spark would pass between them, a hidden promise of the flames of passion that awaited them later.

***

It was 6:00 PM, and Mindy decided to head over to B.'s penthouse. She had picked up a few things from the market, along with a nice bottle of white wine, so that they could make dinner together. It was starting to get dark around the edges of the sky, and Mindy was walking to his house, having gotten rid of her car. It was indeed a bit of a walk, but it was a pleasant night and Mindy was grateful for the exercise. She was dressed in a light, filmy black sweater, a pale pink scoop-neck shirt, and a black skirt. Luckily, her shoes were comfortable enough to walk in. With a smile on her face, Mindy thought about the black lace underwear she was wearing, another surprise for B. She knew his eyes would glow with liquid fire as he stripped it off of her. She couldn't wait to be in his arms again, how he smelled like Arabica coffee and the heart of summer itself…

Mindy was so absorbed in her dreamy thoughts that she didn't hear the crunch of tires on the gravel as a sleek black limo pulled up beside her.

Looking over, Mindy was puzzled as to why the vehicle was slowing to a stop. Just then, the back door opened and out stepped Troy Haverman, looking smug and satisfied with himself, clad in an expensive outfit, complete with nauseating cologne. His polished appearance was somewhat offset by his shaggy ponytail, but the effects combined were enough to inspire vomiting. "Enjoying your vacation, Miss Cullen?" Troy drawled, giving Mindy a lazy once-over.

Mindy was stunned. "What are you doing here?" she demanded forcefully, trying to appear unfazed by his presence.

Troy leered at her. "I've come to collect you," he announced. "It seems you've been playing around up here far too long. Now, if you'll kindly come with me…"

Mindy shook her head. "I've got somewhere else to be. If you'll excuse me," she said coldly. She tried to step around him but before she knew it, Troy had grabbed her arm in an iron grip. Roughly, he spun her around to face him.

"I can't have you gone from work any longer," he growled. Looking her over, he grabbed her bottom and squeezed, and then slapped her hard. "And I can't let any other man have this ass."

Furious, Mindy struggled to slap him back. "Let me go, you buffoon!" she fumed, trying to wrench herself free of his grasp. She hollered for help, but the street was deserted. She had yelled out only once when Troy jammed his meaty hand over her mouth and forced her into the back of the limo, slamming the door.

"So your answer to this is kidnapping me?" Mindy demanded incredulously after Troy had closed the door and ordered the driver to go. "I'm sure that's a great way to take me back to work."

Troy smiled patronizingly. "I'm not kidnapping you," he replied in an oily tone. "I prefer to call it… encouragement. Besides, you aren't going back to work at the bank. I intend to keep you as my mistress, in my mansion." He pressed a button and a wall slid up, barring them from the driver. Then, he tied her hands behind her back, leaned over and began to kiss her neck and tear at her clothes. "I thought we could have some fun while we waited," he purred. "Don't worry, you can scream as loud as you want. The limo is soundproof."

Mindy was panicked. There was no way anyone would be able to rescue her now. Troy had clearly gone out of his mind, and there was no telling what he'd do with her. And once they left the city she would never see B. again, and maybe never see anyone again. Then, she thought of B. and hoped that he would be in city form so he could help her. *Please help me, Burlington,* she pleaded softly.

Startled by her soft murmur, Troy drew back. "What?" he asked sharply.

At that moment, a monumental thunderclap rent the air and torrents of rain began to pound down from above, obliterating all visibility. Mindy felt B.'s presence in the storm. He had heard her plea for help!

Looking out the window, Troy grimaced. He slid down the divider and leaned forward to talk to the driver. "Keep going," he muttered. "I want to get out of this city as soon as possible."

The driver looked bewildered. "I can't see, Mr. Haverman," he pointed out. "It's a straight sheet of water. Maybe we should pull over for a while, wait it out…"

Troy's face turned red and he shook the man by the shoulder. "No," he growled. "Go!"

The driver swallowed nervously and gingerly pressed the accelerator. "As you wish, Mr. Haverman," he said.

Troy slid the wall back up. "Ah, Mindy, I've wanted you since the day I saw you," he said mockingly, running his finger over her sweater. "And all you've done is throw it in my face, make me feel like less than a man. But not anymore, precious, you're mine."

Mindy narrowed her eyes at him. "If you think I'm impressed, you're wrong."

Troy's jaw tightened in rage and he looked like he was about to reply when a commotion outside interrupted. At once, a brilliant flash of lightning singed through the air, illuminating the bleak night like a football stadium and sharply splitting a tree in half. Seconds later, there was a hollow, sonorous crash as the tree fell across the road, and a jarring bump as the limo plowed into it.

"Jesus Christ!" Troy swore. He rolled down the partition. "What's the matter with you, you moron?" he raged at the driver. He shook his fist. "Why did you have to hit that tree?"

"I'm afraid we have a flat tire, sir," the driver said meekly. "I'll get out and check it."

"Absolutely not, you dimwit!" Troy bellowed. "I'll do it myself!"

Now that the damage was done, the thunderstorm cleared away and only a light drizzle remained. Mindy could see the two men bending over the tire, which was indeed ruptured from hitting the tree. While they were out there,

Mindy strained at her bonds, trying to free her wrists from the heavy cords that bound them.

While she was looking out the window, Mindy saw B. sprinting through the mist, a cop car in tow behind him. He looked valiant and strong, and seemed to be almost glowing. She finally got her bonds off and opened the limo door. "B!" she called, going forth to him.

But Troy grabbed her arm once more and attempted to shove her back into the limo. "Not so fast, you little bi-," he growled.

There was a blur of activity and Troy's sentence broke off as B. swung, nailing Troy right in the mouth. The impact was so forceful that Troy was knocked off of his feet and fell face down on the concrete, his lip bleeding heavily. The officers came forward and one read rights to a groaning, barely-conscious Troy while the other one fastened handcuffs on his wrists.

Breathing heavily, his hair damp and hands still glowing, B. turned to Mindy. She could feel his heart pounding and the waves of energy radiating off of him. "Are you all right?" he asked hoarsely.

"I am now," Mindy breathed, looking at him with pure admiration. She clasped his hands in hers. "You're so amazing," she whispered.

"That sonovabitch is gonna have a split lip for quite some time," B. said with a grin. "I could have hit him harder, too."

Mindy looped her arms around B.'s neck, breathing in his rain-soaked scent. He held her for several minutes before he gently pulled away. "Let me take you home," he murmured.

Mindy grinned at him. "I sure could use a nice hot shower," she said seductively, batting her eyelashes.

B.'s gaze turned hot and he slung his arm around her shoulders, leading her to his truck, which was parked a ways back. "If you keep it up, Araminta, we'll never make it home," he murmured in her ear.

"Doesn't matter, Burlington," Mindy whispered, kissing him softly. "Home is with you."

Epilogue

A few weeks later:

It was a gray, cloudy afternoon in mid-November, and Mindy and B. were standing by the window at B.'s penthouse, looking out over the city. Mindy thought about how her life had changed, how she had started over. She had quit her job in New Jersey, and abandoned her old life like releasing a sandbag from a hot air balloon. She had just left everything there, never to return, and pledged to spend her life in the city she loved, with the man she loved.

"I can't believe how quickly the season has changed," Mindy remarked softly. In just a few short weeks, the landscape had changed from the vibrant beauty of Indian summer to the barren stillness of November. The trees were bare, their spindly branches waving in the wind, and the land was hued in gray, orange, and brown. The sky was a light gray as well, and the light snowflakes falling from the strata matched the rhythmic swishing of the waves against Lake Champlain's shore.

B. turned to look at Mindy. "I have a harsh winter, Araminta," he warned her. "But I'll do my best to make it pleasant for you."

Mindy noticed the drawn look on B.'s face and she leaned on his shoulder. "I want your winter, Burlington," she whispered, gathering him into her arms. "I want to be with you every day. Summer or winter, rain or shine, with you every season is beautiful. I just hope I can be enough for you…"

B.'s eyes turned misty, and Mindy saw all of him at once, his summer, his winter, his past and present. The air between them grew taut with dancing electrons, and everything came together as B. crushed his lips to hers.

Mindy's head swam and she closed her eyes, blindly, languidly swimming through the inferno that was their passion. Mindy felt B.'s soft, skilled lips on hers, his hot, hard frame holding her, and most of all she felt him, in her, around her, everywhere. The wind grew into a flowing gale outside, and a plume of brilliantly colored red leaves rose swirling into the air as their now became forever.

The End

If you enjoyed My Sweet Vermont, look at:

Lost & Found

By: Sara J. Kuhrman

Practical, impatient secretary Cindy Washek has always bumbled her way through life, stubborn and surefooted as a mule. But when she finds a woman's purse in the grocery store, she has no idea how it will change her life.

When she goes to return the purse to its owner, she is immediately struck like lightning by the mysterious, dark-haired authoress Teela Grant. The two women become friends, and soon Cindy finds herself falling deeply, completely in love.

Cindy soon learns that Teela harbors dark scars and secrets, and that she is constantly on the run from the shadowy terrors of her past. As these evils begin to reemerge, Cindy finds her strength and wits tested past the limit as she fights to defend herself and frail, restless Teela from their enemies. When the harrowing danger reaches its fever pitch, Cindy must carry out a dramatic rescue… and prove to Teela that love conquers all.

*Available on Amazon.com

Tempest's Bachelor

By: Sara J. Kuhrman

Dreamy, independent Emily Bentley has always preferred a long walk in the woods over a fancy-dress ball. She has no use for the rules of society, and is adamant that she doesn't need or want a husband.

Everything changes the moment Emily lays eyes on earthy, stoic former Navy captain Burley Haven. Floored by his raw strength and intrigued by his distant, thoughtful nature, Emily shyly ventures forth to peel away his iron reserve, falling deeply in love with him along the way.

But Burley has scars, a lifetime of them, and he won't let anyone close to his heart. The sea still haunts his dreams at night, and only Emily's exotic, innocent touch will calm the storm. Together, they must learn to love and trust each other before it is too late.

*Coming soon in 2016

THE HALLOWED HALLS

By Sara J. Kuhrman

Meagan Lucien has always had to fight for what she wants, often having to be reckless to the point of callousness. The only way that she can hide the pain of her past is by fulfilling her every desire. So, when she develops an insatiable attraction to her sexy, charismatic calculus professor, Terrence Reid, naturally she pursues with all of her might.

But when a tragedy strikes in Terrence's family, things change drastically for both of them. Terrence withdraws and blames himself for what happened, and Meagan becomes a social outcast, maturing and learning a lot about herself in the process. Will their lives be consumed in the web of deceit and tragedy or can they find the light at the end of the tunnel?

*Available on Amazon.com

About the Author

Sara J. Kuhrman is a witty, eccentric young lady who is known for always making her own way in life. She loves writing, especially melodramatic stories of people bonding in spite of tragedy or criticism. In her free time, Sara enjoys reading, taking walks and analyzing the ways of the world, always dreaming up another story line.

www.ingramcontent.com/pod-product-compliance
Lightning Source LLC
Chambersburg PA
CBHW060221180626
46813CB00007B/2914